C K JORDAN

A Personal Agenda

A Highlands and Islands Detective Thriller

Carpetless

This book was professionally typeset on Reedsy.
Find out more at reedsy.com

Contents

Foreword

This story is set in the idyllic yet sometimes harsh landscape of the western part of Scotland. Although set amongst known towns and villages, note that all persons and specific places are fictional and not to be confused with actual buildings and structures which have been used as an inspirational canvas to tell a completely fictional story.

Acknowledgement

To Susan, Harold, Evelyn, Pete, Joan, Wendy, Jean and Rosemary for your work in bringing this novel to completion, your time and effort is deeply appreciated.

Novels by G R Jordan

The Highlands and Islands Detective series (Crime)

1. Water's Edge
2. The Bothy
3. The Horror Weekend
4. The Small Ferry
5. Dead at Third Man
6. The Pirate Club
7. A Personal Agenda
8. A Just Punishment

The Patrick Smythe Series

1. The Disappearance of Russell Hadleigh (Crime)
2. The Graves of Calgary Bay
3. The Fairy Pools Gathering

Austerley & Kirkgordon Series (Fantasy)

1. Crescendo!
2. The Darkness at Dillingham
3. Dagon's Revenge
4. Ship of Doom

Supernatural and Elder Threat Assessment Agency (SETAA) Series (Fantasy)

1. Scarlett O'Meara: Beastmaster

Island Adventures Series (Cosy Fantasy Adventure)

1. Surface Tensions

Dark Wen Series (Horror Fantasy)

1. The Blasphemous Welcome
2. The Demon's Chalice

Chapter 1

The small cruise ship had been a great idea and John stood with a satisfied grin on the open deck behind the bar. The kids were not with them, placed with their grandmother for a week, and the peace and quiet was exceptional. It was not that he struggled to love them in any way, it was just that being a busy parent was full on everyday and there was no rest. Alison and he had lost each other in the maelstrom of family life and now they had a chance to rekindle some fires.

The compact cruise ship was ideal, capable of sailing down the Caledonian Canal, taking them along Loch Ness and through Fort Augustus before arriving at the top of Neptune's Staircase. This was a breath-taking series of locks that descended the hillside and would leave the vessel in the canal that led to the sea loch at Fort William. Looking down the locks, he saw other vessels already on their way down the staircase, dropping through each one as the water flowed out.

Alison was showering and he had a gin and tonic ready for her. In fact, he was eagerly awaiting her arrival and the summer dress she had bought for the trip. Today was the first day without cloud and she had laid it out on the bed. Having just turned forty, she was not the youthful girl he had dated and married all those years ago, but she was now something different—even better, he thought, despite the markings life had made on her. In truth she had aged better than he but who really cared when the sun was up and the drink was ready to flow. Tonight would be good night, after a relaxing evening.

Across from John was a German gentleman, named Klaus, who had spoken to John as they cruised along Loch Ness. Recounting the man's tales of the monster, John chuckled inwardly at the German's impression of a hulking beast with a long neck, his arms swinging out before him in something that looked more like a deformed elephant. Still the man had been good company and despite the language barrier, they had enjoyed the view and the tales of Nessie.

A pair of arms slipped around John causing him to smile and he leaned his head back over his shoulder to give a kiss to his wife. Twisting out of her grasp, he gave a delightful look at her dress and even asked her to spin for him. A German voice from behind echoed his enthusiasm and John handed Alison her gin, stepping with her to the railing at the edge of the deck.

'How long will it take us to go down this staircase?' asked Alison.

'Most of the evening, I reckon. Why? You going somewhere?'

'Only with you.' She took his hand and he ignored the cheesy comment and simply smiled. She did not have a way with words but that had never bothered him as her sentiments were always real. John invited Alison to sit but she insisted on standing at the railing and looking out over the town of Fort William below. Away to their left, John could see the impressive Ben Nevis and was glad he did not have time to climb it, despite Alison's protests. He wanted all their physical activity to be in the bedroom and now looking at the landmark, he thought he could never make it that high up a mountain. Even with a cable car, he still found himself not relishing a walk.

But Alison was looking on the other side, staring over trees that lined the staircase onto a rugby field and to the hills in the background. And then she stood back a little, almost reeling, as if she had seen something.

'You okay?' asked John.

'Sorry, I just thought I'd seen a man with a gun. Well, more like the nozzle of a rifle. Just walking along down there.'

'Where?' asked John, more to entertain Alison's fantastical idea than in any sort of apprehension.

'It was that man … oh, blast he's gone. I'm sure he was down there.'

'Probably just a trick of the light; the sun's getting pretty low. Here, get some of this down you.'

'Now, John,' said Alison with a smile, 'you're not trying to get me drunk so you can get me back into bed, are you?'

'Of course,' he laughed.

'I don't need to be drunk, trust me.'

The pair kissed like they were teenagers, without a care for anyone staring at them and John even reached round, placing his hands on Alison's bottom. When they broke, he watched her take the glass to her lips and drink it quickly.

'Here's to getting me pissed!'

'It going to be a good night, ja!' said Klaus.

'The best,' said John and embraced his wife again.

A deafening crack was heard and behind their heads a light smashed on the facia above their deck. Instinctively, John ducked before turning to look at the broken fixture which had rained plastic onto the deck.

3

'Blimey, I didn't realise you were that explosive, Ali.' His wife giggled and held him tight.

'Take it easy,' said Klaus; 'we want a ship by the end of tonight, not a smashed up one.'

John grinned but then jumped as another thunderous crack rocketed through the air and a piece of plastic facia blew apart above Klaus' head. This time John was not smiling, and he began to panic.

'Gun—it's a gun,' screamed Alison.

Behind Klaus, a waiter was yelling at the guests to get inside when he suddenly spun and fell off his feet to the floor. Blood began to seep onto his white shirt and a nearby passenger quickly knelt down and began turning him over, looking for a wound.

'I'm a doctor. Keep down and get off the deck.'

A third shot broke more of the facia above them and John heard screams from those strolling along the canal bank on what had been a perfect evening. John pulled his mobile from his pocket and dialled 999.

'What service do you require?'

'Police, get me the damn police; there's shooting—someone shooting at us!'

'Putting you through,' came the calm voice of the operator.

John then heard a broken voice, dropping in and out. Blasted signal, he thought and gingerly stood up trying to raise the height of his phone. As he did, another shot rang out and John felt his arm being pulled away from him, but he manged to steady it. Then in a delayed reaction, he felt pain shooting from his hand and looked to see a destroyed mobile phone in his hand. But he nearly puked when he saw only three fingers on his hand. Blood began to pour from the knuckles and he

4

heard Alison scream.

For a moment everything reeled, and he looked over at Klaus who was kneeling behind the railing, taking cover behind the solid body of the vessel. For a moment he saw Klaus hesitate, as if there was something he should be doing but was unsure of. And then the man stood up and began walking over to John.

'No,' John mumbled, his voice gone from him as his head felt woozy. But he manged to raise his left arm, indicating that Klaus should go back. Another thunderous sound and this time, John saw Klaus lifted off his feet, his head violently twisting backwards as he fell and blood spattering all around. Lying there, John watched the man's head turn towards him as it hit the deck, one eye missing and the other without life. Klaus' face was almost unrecognizable, and John felt the bile in his throat rise up before a little came out. Behind him, Alison was not so reserved and vomited profusely.

'Stay down,' John mumbled, unsure if he was echoing his instruction to Klaus or instructing his wife. Lying there, he saw the doctor still working on the waiter and others now crawling along the deck to reach Klaus. On the deck where the fading sun could not get past the height of the railings, it was cool, and a coldness set in on him. Whether this was real or a result of his wounds or shock, John was in no position to debate, but instead he simply stared at his recent German friend whose teeth had now formed a vague smile as he lay on the ground.

On the top deck of the vessel, the crew manning the control room were all lying on the ground lest they were exposed by the glass wall that gave such excellent visibility. Many now thought that guiding a vessel by radar was preferable and they could be safely locked in, keeping low on the bridge. The captain was holding a microphone in his hands, simply calling out 'Mayday' as another crew member rang 999 on the ship's mobile. Another pressed the secret button which would send an email message indicating distress and possible attack. But every crewman did these things hugging the floor.

John lay where he was, slowly drifting away from the scene around him. Somewhere, he heard the sound of a bird, a shrill cry, and he wallowed in this, wondering what it looked like. Who cared what had happened; this was a most beautiful sound. The ideal was broken by his wife, slapping his face, asking him if he was okay. But John was struggling to speak and she screamed again.

But as the sound of people scurrying about attending to screaming passengers filed the air, there was an ominous silence from the gun. Had it gone? Was the shooting over? John wondered this as he drifted off, wishing he could hear that bird again.

Chapter 2

Macleod watched the woman on his patio staring out at the Moray Firth. She was bald and he noticed that she had those ears that stick out. Usually they would have been covered by thick hair that rolled in waves to her shoulders. But that beauty was gone, as she frequently commented. He had told her it would return again but that had made things worse. He did not know why, in fact, from Macleod, it was an unusually positive outlook, but not for Hazel.

Hazel Mackintosh had moved into Macleod's home after returning from Glasgow and the cancer treatment that had changed her physically forever. Macleod had no idea how to approach the subject the first time he saw her, after the tumultuous case in Barra. He still struggled to mention anything about it but Jane had known what to say. His partner had been incredibly compassionate considering Hazel was a woman with an eye for Macleod. But there was no hidden agenda with cancer, only pain.

A hand was placed on Macleod's shoulder. 'She's doing okay, as well as can be expected. You're a heck of a good man letting her stay.'

He placed his hand on Jane's and kept staring at Mackintosh's back. 'You're the good one, knowing how she feels about me.'

'Well, you can't blame her; she doesn't know you like me. I've made my mistake and she doesn't have to.'

'That's wicked.' Macleod managed a grin and rolled himself around Jane eventually holding her from behind. 'How long do you think she'll be here?'

'As long as she needs, Seoras. The woman's had one of the worst things happen to her I can imagine, so she can stay for as long as she needs.'

'You're something else, Jane.' He hugged her tight but then suddenly let go as Mackintosh began to turn around. Wondering if she saw, he heard the telephone ring and turned away immediately to answer it. 'Yes, Macleod here.'

'Stewart, sir. There's been a gun attack at Fort William. Some lunatic has let off a number of shots and a German's been killed, sir. DCI wants you over there as soon as possible. I'm at the station in Inverness; shall I come get you?'

'Yes, Stewart, I'll be ready. Do you have cover for your brother?'

'Yes, sir. We have an arrangement in place so Alasdair, the carer, will be over. I'll see you shortly.'

'Where?' asked Jane as soon as Macleod put the telephone down.

'Fort William. Someone's shot a German. Hopefully, it won't be that long.'

'Don't say that; you know how these things go. I'm under no illusions. Besides, I have my patient.'

'I hope I'm a guest and not simply a patient,' said Mackintosh, coming in through the patio doors.

'A friend, Hazel,' said Macleod. 'But I have to run. Someone's been shot in Fort William, so you two ladies will have to take care of each other.' Macleod saw the hunger in Mackintosh's eyes, the desire to race to the latest scene. He wondered if there really was anything else in her life; certainly nothing had come up in their conversations. Such a pity for the woman.

'Tell Jona I'm on the phone if she needs anything.'

'I will, Hazel, but she's doing well—clever girl.'

'You can't say that these days, Seoras, even if she is nearly thirty years younger than us.' Mackintosh smiled and nudged Jane. 'He can't help it—sees them all as kids.'

'Well, they are compared to us, Hazel, even Hope.' Macleod saw the look on Mackintosh's face and the tears forming in the eyes.

'You'll be back, Hazel; trust me.'

'Don't make promises you can't cash, Seoras.' The forensic chief turned away and walked back out to the patio, resuming her observations of the Moray Firth.

'Not your fault,' said Jane; 'that's her battle to believe. Now get your stuff and get out of here, Inspector Macleod. Go sort those young ones out.'

'Yes, ma'am,' said Macleod and gave his partner a hug before heading for the stairs to his bedroom.

The drive to Fort William took Macleod along the Caledonian Canal where the sun blazed on the water. On passing the Loch Ness centre, he saw the mass of tourists all desperate for a glimpse of the elusive monster. 'Why would you spend your money on something that's not even real?' he asked Stewart.

'Day out, sir. Keeps the kids happy.'

'Look at that couple; they don't even have kids.'

'No sir, they're having fun though. Maybe that's worth the money.'

Macleod watched a hand rise and the glasses on Stewart's

face were pushed back as they always were when she thought she had made a winning point. He was about to complain about a lack of respect for elders when he realised that he had been complaining about people's holiday plans. He was moaning more and more these days, in a return to his days of bitterness in Glasgow. He'd have to stop that. Hazel's troubles were bringing him down.

The car crossed the bridge at the Ben Nevis Distillery and Macleod knew he was close to the canal's end. Once they had crossed the bridge over the canal, Stewart swung the car round in the now-dying sunshine and drove up the side of the canal past a mass of emergency vehicles. The path was only infrequently used by vehicles but today it was like a car showroom. Parking up when they could get no further forward, Macleod exited the car and flashed his warrant card at the constable manning the cordon.

'Up there, sir. I can see McGrath with Ross.' Macleod followed Stewart's direction and saw his sergeant who was talking with a uniformed officer. Macleod walked briskly towards her but started to feel the heat of the day as he climbed uphill, dressed in his full suit.

'McGrath, situation report, please.'

'Yes, sir, and good to see you, too.' Macleod ignored the jibe. 'We believe someone stood approximately here, took a number of shots with a high-powered rifle towards the *Lord of the Isles*, a pleasure boat which was descending Neptune's Staircase, or at least the second lock. He missed with all but two shots. One took the fingers off a tourist and the other killed a German holiday maker. I've had London on the phone worried that it was a terrorist attack but in truth, there's been nothing in the media or anyone claiming it as an attack. And if it was, it's a damn shoddy one.'

'There are a number of witnesses, sir,' said Ross, 'but the gunman was wearing a hoodie and no one saw his face. We're still interviewing and getting addresses. The German is still on board with forensics working on the scene. Jona Nakamura's running point on that. The other injured party was taken to the local hospital. They were thinking of trying to save his fingers initially, but they were too smashed up to be reattached in any meaningful way. He was in the hospital in Fort William but they moved him to Glasgow.'

'Anyone get a word with him before they moved him?'

'No, sir,' said Hope, 'but I have two constables down there getting a statement from the wife. Everyone else we have interviewed on the bridge didn't see where the shots came from and generally got down on the deck.'

'Okay, but I want you or Ross down to interview the injured holiday maker and his wife from the point of view of who they are and could they have been a target. Stewart, get the names of the passengers on the vessel and see if there is anyone of note, maybe mistaken identity. Also, there were other boats coming up and down here, so get some details and see if our shooter was so rubbish he was hitting the wrong boat.'

'Sir!' said Stewart and took off.

'I'm going to see Miss Nakamura—see what light she can shed. But I want a roundup of the statements from the bystanders and an idea of what happened down here. That's your priority, Ross. McGrath, you're running with our German fatality. Who is he? Find the others who were with him. Why him? Why our fingerless man as well?'

Macleod went to walk off and then stopped. He took off his jacket and handed it to Ross. 'Here, find a safe home for this.

11

Too warm for a day like this.'

Ross looked at McGrath as Macleod walked off up the hillside and past the various locks that comprised the staircase. The Caledonian Canal ended and started at Fort William but there was a climb from the sea loch up to the narrow canal that led to Loch Lochy. In the summer it was a busy route for tourists and sailing boats as the canal took you all the way up to Loch Ness and Inverness where you could sail out into the Moray firth. The large pleasure cruiser that was involved was well known to Macleod and he had seen it several times at Inverness, but he never imagined an attack on it.

The vessel was floating in between two locks and there was a gangway rigged up to the vessel from the canal side. Macleod flashed his warrant card at the constable and proceeded onto the vessel and walked towards the foredeck where the German man had died. From a distance, he saw Jona Nakamura, diminutive in stature but totally in charge, organising her people with total confidence.

'Hazel sends her best and says she's available if you need her on the phone. I told her you were too good for help.' Macleod saw her grin at the compliment and then looked at him with a face of concern.

'How is she?'

'Struggling, Jona. But she has perfect faith in you. So, tell me what you have.'

'Our victim was shot by a high-powered rifle with a shot to the head, probably killing him instantly. The shots were pretty wild as several parts of the facia above the deck were hit and shattered. I'm working on the trajectories of the bullets but according to DS McGrath, the shooter was quite far down the steps and that would be consistent with the initial look at the bullet paths. However, I will get a more accurate picture for you, sir, in case we had a second unsighted shooter. We are trying to look along the canal side for any evidence, but to be honest, by the time the emergency services raced up the path and the general public scattered over it, there's going to be a complete mess. But we will look.'

'Good, keep me updated.'

'One thing, sir,' said Jona. 'I would expect something this high powered to be used by a marksman, someone who could handle it. These shots are really wild, like an amateur, not someone simply having an off-day or even bedding in a new sight or weapon.'

'Are you saying our German friend was a random victim?' asked Macleod.

'No, sir. It may be he was the intended, but it took a few shots to get him. But to pick off someone's hand as they were low down and raising it above the railing, looks like a wild shot. You could not identify the victim before the hand came into sight. Could have been anyone. Also, why shoot from the path? The person was wearing a hoodie and chose to simply stand on the path with a high-powered rifle. There are better weapons to hit someone with if you're prepared to be in the open. A good handgun if you stopped just off the path across from us would work. You'd be just as unidentifiable as if you were further down the path and the weapon could be concealed better.'

'How did they conceal the weapon?'

'You'll need to talk to the team doing the interviews, but it would need to be a reasonable-sized bag, especially as you would need to reveal the weapon, fire, and then stow it and run. No time to assemble or disassemble if you are in the open.

And all the bullet paths suggested every shot was fired from the open path.'

Macleod nodded and stepped off the boat back onto the canal side. Surely it must be a random killing. To have known your victim would be on deck at the front of the vessel would be almost impossible unless you had been in contact. The wildness of the shootings also gave credence that this was an opportunistic killing, or at least a random one.

Macleod's mobile rang and he nearly groaned as he saw the image of his boss. *Give a moment.* 'Macleod here, ma'am.'

'Seoras, just wanted you to know there's going to be a lot of heat on this one. It's your investigation but the terrorist branch down south will be sending someone up. I want full co-operation, sharing of all evidence. They reckon it could be a terrorist incident.'

'Well, if it is, ma'am, it's a weird one. Solo with a high-powered rifle, not from the shadows and wearing a hoodie for cover. Victim does appear initially to be a random choice. It just doesn't have the terrorist feel, and why Fort William? It's very random choice. They also could have shot numerous people on the canal path but no one there was even injured. Extremely poor shots, too—very amateur.'

'Nonetheless, when their man gets there, full co-operation.'

'Of course, ma'am.'

'I'll let you get on, Seoras; keep me posted.'

Macleod closed down the call and stood looking from beside the boat past the other vessels trapped in between the various locks and where he saw Hope talking to various uniformed officers. *They could have caused a bloodbath here. But they didn't, instead only one dead, one injured, and damage to a boat. Why target this vessel? Something was wrong about the whole incident.*

Macleod rolled up his shirt sleeves and mopped sweat from his brow. Walking down to where he saw Ross, Macleod kept looking back at the vessel, Jona's words ringing in his head about how it would be easier to shoot at the vessel from closer up with a different weapon. There had been no distraction tactics either. And where had he gone afterwards?

'Ross,' called Macleod and his DC came over. 'What are the initial descriptions of the shooter?'

Ross pulled out a notebook. Maybe five feet-five to five feet-ten, usual selection from the public. Wearing a red hoodie with the hood up. It was big for him, kept his face covered. Jeans, blue with a belt, black. Hiking boots on, brown ones. Carried a large bag, triangular in shape, they said. Here, I had one do a sketch.'

Macleod looked down at the pencil drawing and saw a bag that was like a triangle with curved sides running to the apex. The zip ran through the apex allowing a whole side of the bag to open and give easy access to the contents. But it was not narrow enough for a gun bag.

'Anyone know what sort of bag that is? Did it have a brand name on it?'

'Easton,' said Ross; 'I don't recognise it.'

'Google it now.'

Ross took out his mobile and Macleod waited for the result of the search. He would have done it himself except he was a philistine on the mobile testified to by the various hot keys and pictures of contacts Hope had programmed onto it.

'Archery suppliers, sir.'

'Clever enough not to use a gun bag and alert people. Where did the shooter go, Ross?'

'General consensus from the bystanders was that he ran into

the car park near the bottom of the staircase and then vanished. We're still trying to see if anyone clocked a car, or him getting into one.'

'Okay, Ross, one other thing. Why him? Do we have anything to say positively it was a male shooter?'

Ross nodded. 'Witnesses said male; several did.'

'Did all say a man?'

'No.'

'Any say a woman?'

'No, sir.'

'Recheck and I want to know why they are saying male if the face was not seen. People's shapes can be similar, male and female.'

Macleod strode down to grab a uniformed sergeant who was running the local uniform response. The woman had a shaved head which unnerved Macleod slightly though he did not know why. Maybe it was having seen Mackintosh go from a full and abundant head of hair to baldness. He never understood why any woman would want to cut her hair, as glorious as it was but then, he rarely understood women. Even when he was being cordial, he could manage to offend.

'Sergeant, DI Macleod. I take it you have local stop and search in progress?' The woman nodded. 'How far out?'

'Five-mile perimeter, sir, but in truth he could have gone before we were set up. Obviously, we came straight here and there's not that many of us for something like this. It's not that common here. We're not London.'

No, thought Macleod, *you're not. So, why here?*

'Detective Inspector Macleod?'

The voice was not asking but searching and Macleod spun around to see a man in his thirties striding along the canal side

16

in a grey suit. He had a mop of blond hair that somehow had a life of its own, looking full and abundant. Macleod could feel a touch of jealousy, his own hair having given up the idea that any colour but black streaked with silver was an option. The man had a crisp cream shirt on and his arms seemed to fill it with bulging muscles. Maybe he was ex-army or simply worked out.

'I'm Macleod, sir. Who are you?'

'Apologies, Inspector, Parry, from Scotland Yard. I'm up here to liaise with you and keep an eye on this from a terrorist perspective. I don't wish to impede you but I was looking for a briefing. I did get an initial one immediately after the incident but was looking for a bit more depth as you have it.'

Macleod stepped forward and held out a hand. A vice-like grip took him and he was delighted to break the handshake. Looking around him, he saw Ross and Hope and called them over.

'These are my colleagues, DS McGrath and DC Ross.' Macleod saw the man's eyes flash across them both and then come back briefly to Hope before he extended a hand. 'There's also DC Stewart who's on the vessels in the locks interviewing. Any of them can fill you in on the details of what's happening. And team, Mr Parry is to be afforded full disclosure; he's from London and the terrorist branch. Feel free to use him as a sounding post, too.'

Macleod mopped his brow and noted the man was barely sweating. 'Maybe DS McGrath could give me a brief?' Parry asked.

'Sorry, Mr Parry, but I need McGrath right now. Ross will show you around and that. Introduce him to Miss Nakamura too, Ross; make sure she knows his status.'

'Thanks, Inspector. I'll see you shortly after Ross fills me in.' Macleod watched the pair depart but also noted the glance back from Parry at Hope. Macleod grinned inwardly. If he had pitched up, he would have looked for Hope to have briefed him as well.

'You needed me, sir?'

Macleod turned to Hope. 'No, but you're a sergeant now; you don't need to be holding anyone's hand.' He saw her laugh before walking back to her job.

Macleod stood and looked around him at the scene. *What was this? Terrorist? Nutter? Some unknown feud?* One thing was for sure, these holiday makers would never forget Neptune's Staircase.

Chapter 3

The community centre just outside Fort William was close to the canal and was an ideal base to run operations from while keeping the main Fort William station free from the palaver that accompanied an incident of this magnitude. Macleod had been studying statements in an attempt to find out more about the killer but the trouble with the general public was that they often collectively produced a general assessment and not a specific one. But Hope had sourced some CCTV footage and was scanning it now.

There came a knock on his office door, a small room at the back of the facility but one of the few where he could get any peace and quiet. After a moment, Stewart stuck her head round the door and Macleod waved her in.

'I hope you have something because these witness statements are just not going anywhere.'

'Yes, sir,' said Stewart, 'but I'm not sure I'm going to be that much help either. The dead man was Klaus Schneider, on holiday with his wife, Mia. They had been touring in a car before catching passage on the small cruise ship. Worth a bit of money but no one special, sir. Mr Parry got in contact with his German equivalents and they have nothing untoward on him either. Wrong time, wrong place by the looks of it.'

'What about our injured man?'

Stewart pushed her glasses back. 'Well, name of John Green, from Sussex. His wife Alison had just come onto deck as it happened. Neither have any record or been involved in any terrorist or gangland activity. He runs some horse stables in a few counties. Bit of money but again nothing special. She's a horse trainer. I can't find any reason for someone to shoot them either. In fact, of those on the deck at the time of shooting I have nothing. Even the surrounding boats, I only have one ex-con but he's been straight twenty years and was on a boat that was out of the line of fire.'

'Okay, Stewart, good work. Looks like it might have been a nutter but keep the nose to the grindstone. Close the door, will you?'

Stewart looked at him but then closed the door as asked.

'With regard to your anxiety issues around chasing suspects and engaging in confrontation, are the sessions helping? I don't need detail; I just need to know where you are at for operational reasons.' Macleod watched Stewart shift in her seat. 'Kirsten, I need to know what situation I can put you in. It's not just about you—it's about protecting the team as well.'

'Well, sir, it is going well but I still think I'll react badly in pursuit especially if they turn at me. I've been back in the MMA ring at the gym and that's no problem but it's a different environment. I'm still getting the nightmares.'

Macleod thought back to the incident in Newcastle where Stewart had almost been killed. Only the intervention of a second suspect, who had then been killed for his actions, had prevented her death. It was no wonder she was having trouble reconciling this. The crazy thing was she was much better placed to handle herself than Macleod was, if someone turned on them.

'I'll bear it in mind, Kirsten. But any issues, make sure you let me know. I don't want to compromise you or anyone else on the team.'

'Of course not, sir. I'll get back to it.'

As Stewart opened the door, Hope came in and plonked herself on the seat in front of Macleod. 'CCTV,' she paused and checked behind her making sure the door was closed, 'Seoras. I can tell you that our suspect is actually around five feet five and wore a red hoodie and blue jeans with hiking boots. But as to whether it's a man or a woman, you can't tell. Certainly not a busty woman. Even a girl my size would show in a hoodie like that.'

Macleod tried not to imagine the image and think if Hope was right, instead deciding to take her word for it. 'And the rest of the build?'

'Again, male or female. No beefcake but an average man could be in those clothes or a small breasted female. Sorry, but I can't tell. On the bright side, we managed to find out which car they took when they ran off.'

'Did you put the call out for it?' asked Macleod.

'Of course, Seoras, but it was found burning, nearly nothing left of it. Just across from Locheilside Railway Station. Checking the train footage now. But according to my constable looking at it, he can't find the suspect boarding the train, never mind where they got off.'

'Maybe they didn't get on, a bit of misdirection. Check taxi firms in case they picked up from there. But they might have done and not known. I bet the hoodie is in that burning car.'

'You think this person is that well planned, Seoras?'

Macleod stood up and walked over to a small window that

21

looked out to the hills that surrounded them. 'It feels wrong if the point were to attack and kill. They had a high-powered rifle, loads of people about, yet chose to shoot at a boat which was miles away compared to the bystanders. And then they had a car to run to and drive off. They burn the evidence; they keep themselves hidden with the over-sized hoodie. This was not a half-arsed attempt at terror. And we cannot find anyone who could be on a killer's list in the vicinity. Something is looking me in the face, and I can't see it.'

'Well, if it waves at you let me know because I can't get it at all. By the way, Parry wants to buy us all dinner.'

'When? Two a.m. Really, Hope, we're not going to be out of here any time soon.'

'Nice of him though. Jona's the only person who's bought me dinner since I split with Allinson.' Macleod saw a mournful look on Hope's face before she forced a smile. 'I was kind of hoping for a wee break.'

'Tell him to get a carryout for about nine. And none of that cheap kebab stuff and that. Proper curry or Chinese. He can probably afford it on a London wage.'

Hope laughed and left the room. Macleod dropped a quick call to Jane, basically saying hello and yes, he was really busy. He asked about Mackintosh, but the news was not good. The woman was struggling. Hanging up the call, Macleod felt he was in an easier place than his partner. Walking to the door of the small makeshift office, he opened it and surveyed the hall outside.

Stewart was sitting behind a desk, laptop open and concentrating hard on the screen. When she had first worked with him, he felt she had a knack for sniffing out details with solid investigation, ferreting away until the truth came out. Ross was walking about amongst the uniformed constables making sure everything was checked and processed, ever thorough. And then there was Hope—attractive as ever, he could not deny that but now she was also a colleague he had grown to know and respect. If he did not make her the best DI the force would ever have, then it would not be his fault. After initial friction, he had a team that worked and that operated extremely well together.

True, they were a bit broken, held together by a mixture of care, passion, and sheer bloody mindedness, but they were his team. And with his home life being as good as it had been in the last twenty years, he was a satisfied man. More than that, he was on top of his game and that's why he had this case. The boss would not have handed this to just anyone.

The door at the far end of the hall opened and Macleod saw Jona Nakamura march in wearing a red t-shirt and jeans. She was usually better attired but in fairness, the woman had been in a coverall suit all day and must be dying for a shower. But instead, she was here to update him. Mackintosh had trained her well and if Hazel did not make it back to full time work then Miss Nakamura would be an ideal replacement.

Replacement. He hated the word. Hazel was not someone you just replaced. Over the last months he had become extremely fond of Hazel and he wondered if not for the wonderful woman that his partner was, would they have become even closer. Now she was suffering and struggling with the alterations that surgery had made to her body; he found himself not just with greater admiration for Mackintosh but actually feeling more for the woman. But he was never tempted to exceed the care he could give. Jane was too precious for that.

Jona had arrived at Macleod's office and was standing in front of him. Macleod was unsure how long she had been there, for he saw her come in and then had drifted. The woman was unbelievably polite, simply standing there, waiting for Macleod to finish his private thoughts. Stewart or Ross would have given a warning cough. Hope would have told him to wake up.

'Miss Nakamura, come in,' said Macleod, opening the door and offering a seat to his Asian colleague.

'I have reports on the weapon, sir, and a bit more.'

'Good,' said Macleod. 'Update me now and then I'll bring the room to attention for you.' Jona looked at him. 'So you can brief them. I know McGrath or myself would normally but it's a forensic update and it will boost your standing amongst the uniforms and my team. And you can answer the difficult questions rather than me taking notes to get back to you with.'

Jona smiled and took her seat, placing a file on the desk. 'First off, sir, it's a custom build based on a Remington. You don't simply buy that off the shelf here in the UK, but you can in other countries. However, they got it, that's what it is, and it's had homemade modifications. I'll give Stewart the specifications that I can see so she can trawl and see if anything's been bought or sold recently on the underground markets, but it'll be a long shot for you.'

'How good do you need to be to operate it?'

'Well, that's the thing. It's a rifle you can start with and modify to your own specification.'

'So, our shooter was simply a poor marksman?'

Jona shook her head. 'Not necessarily. Like all weapons, especially those you would operate for distance shooting, you need to tune it to yourself. The reason for the distance the suspect walked, sir, in order to start making those shots, would have been because his target would have been too close. A handgun or something blunter would have been better at short distance. This weapon is for shooting at a bit of distance. I have no doubt the boat was his target even if he's not wielding his weapon right yet.'

Macleod stood up. 'So, we have what? Some rank amateur having a go, or someone who's just off their game?'

'Given he doesn't settle to shoot—that's assume a prone position—he actually doesn't do that badly.'

'But, Jona, he could not have known that the passengers he hit would have been on that deck at that time.'

'Sir, maybe the boat was the target. Maybe that was why he was not worried about precision.'

The Inspector walked out from behind his desk causing the forensic officer to spin in her chair. Macleod placed a hand on the wall and leaned on it, before looking back at her. 'Jona, is it possible for a woman to operate a weapon like this? Could it have been a matter of strength that caused the shots to be off?'

Jona Nakamura furrowed her face and Macleod was confused about what she was thinking. 'Sit down please, sir.' Macleod took his seat with a confused face. 'Now arm out and I want you to wrestle mine to the desk.'

Jona had her hand out, elbow to the table, ready for an arm wrestle. Macleod was bemused as he looked at his colleague with her lesser frame. She had that slim build not uncommon amongst her people and her hands looked delicate compared to his. Macleod placed his own elbow on the table and took up her hand with his.

'You ready?' he asked.

'Whenever you want to start, sir. And don't hold back.'

Gently, Macleod applied a small amount of pressure but found Jona's hand to be solid. Slowly, he increased the force used but her hand never budged. Not being the strongest man around and past his physical prime, Macleod had nonetheless seen Miss Nakamura as a poor challenge at best. It was not so. He began to sweat a little but still nothing. Now he placed everything into it.

'You are, in general, physically stronger than us, but there is little you can do we cannot, in a matter of strength. There's not the gap most men expect. Unless the man's name is Clark Kent, some woman somewhere will match him for strength. And even he had a cousin.'

The reference went over Macleod's head, but he felt a frustration building up. Jona may be right but he was going to win this challenge. He threw everything into his arm and sought to pin her hand to the table. Without warning, his hand flew backwards and smacked hard onto the surface causing a bang that reverberated around the small room.

Jona let his hand go and said, 'To answer your question, it could have been a woman.'

As if the incident had never happened, Jona quickly detailed the rest of her investigations which in truth were producing nothing of significant note. Sitting there and still sweating, Macleod was amazed at how she was taking no delight in his defeat. Jane would have teased him, albeit in a sweet way, Hope would have mocked him openly if away from the other members of the team, and Ross would have stood there quietly as if nothing was untoward, but underneath he would have been laughing.

When Jona had finished, Macleod took the paperwork she offered and said, 'Five minutes outside; you can run this down

26

for the rest of them. And no theatrics, please.'

Smiling, Jona stood up, turned to the door, but then suddenly swung back. 'May I speak candidly, sir?'

Macleod's heart sunk. Had he insulted another female unwittingly? Surely his brutal defeat in the arm wrestle was punishment enough. 'Of course, Miss Nakamura.'

'Hope, that is McGrath, had warned me that you can be a bit backward in your opinions regarding women. She said you once told her that frontline work was not for women. I get that. Sometimes my culture has strict rules too, or opinions about who should be doing whatever. I guess when you were young, the world and our place in it must have been quite different. But it seems to me you want to protect us. Some of us actually think that's a noble trait, sir. Don't lose it. But maybe don't underestimate us either.'

'I'll do my best, Jona. And by the way, where did you get such a strong arm?'

'I train. When I took on this line of police work, my father had me learn how to protect myself. He was like you, saw himself as a protector of women, certainly his wife and children. But he knew he could not be there all the time and with the line of work I chose, he insisted I take classes. Two years ago, a man tried to force himself on me. I escaped and he was left very sore. My father had protected me. It's a noble trait, sir; use it wisely and you'll protect us all.'

Macleod stood and grabbed the door handle but then stopped. 'Am I okay opening the door for you?' He was in no way mocking her and Jona simply smiled.

'Of course. But I would not do it for McGrath. I actually feel for you at times.' Macleod was taken aback and raised his eyebrows. 'Must be a minefield. How do you know what each

27

of us likes?'

'At least you only get to deal with simple creatures,' Macleod replied, opening the door.

'So we think. My mother thought different.' With that, she exited the room and Macleod saw her lean up against a table and look at the front of the hall, the place she would be standing in a few minutes to brief the team. Jona of a few minutes ago, confident and instructing a senior figure, was now looking somewhat nervous, which baffled Macleod.

I can see why Mackintosh liked her. And his mind swung back to his suffering colleague. *It's never all roses, is it?*

Chapter 4

Peter Chesterton strode across the first section of the Skye Bridge with his rucksack slung over his shoulder. Last night he had eaten splendidly, a large twelve-ounce steak being at the centre of the meal and he had spent some time watching the waves come ashore at Kyleakin. The bed and breakfast had been recommended by Gloria's friend, that nosey bitch, but she had been right about its ability to deliver first-class service. Definitely a perfect bed to sleep in for your last trip to dreamland.

Before him, he saw the road rise to become the first section of the Skye Bridge. In reality it was two bridges which met at a small island in the middle of the channel between the Isle of Skye and the Scottish mainland. And the first one was not what he wanted. The drop was not exceptionally large, and he might hit the water and begin to swim, when all he wanted was to sink like a stone, without a trace.

The trouble with working in the capital was that you saw some horrific sights. As he was a paramedic, you would have thought blood would not bother him, but it was not so much the blood as the casual brutality of one man to another and then to the very service who had arrived to help. Karen had been stabbed while patching up a member of a gang. But she had been stabbed by his fellow gang member. The poor girl was left scarred and struggled to go out of the house now. And then Gordon, his new colleague, had been beaten up while on duty by a drunk man who Gordon was attending. Sometimes people should be culled. These people were certainly not victims.

But these thoughts would not cloud his day as he strode up the bridge and sought out the position from which he would jump. It would be beyond the island on the second bridge. Good height there and a stunning view. But it was not quite the last view that he wanted but he had decided that Sarah from the local supermarket would not stand and pose for him while he jumped to his doom. She was up for a lot of things but not that.

In his mind, Peter thought about those large hooped earrings Sarah wore with the crop top and the black tight three-quarter leggings. Her family had given him grief and he had been punched by her father. Today was meant to be an age of equality and understanding where you could be who you wanted to be. Well, he had wanted Sarah and she had wanted him. Who cared about the thirty-year gap between them? She was twenty-one after all, able to make up her own mind.

Leah had cared. She had pestered him and hounded him despite being told their marriage was over. She had no understanding of what he wanted, what was important to him. All that cow did was take his money and spend it. When he was having his breakdown, she had not helped but insisted he got back to work, worried about when the sick pay would stop. Back when they had married, she had been a dream but that had faded fast. He would not miss her.

At least the sun was working on his behalf today and he felt the punishing rays beginning to pick up on his neck. He had not rushed today, instead taking an hour over his breakfast and then calling Sarah, face timing her so he could see her for one last time. In fact, she'd been quite naughty in the call which was perfect. Everything had lined up exactly right for his exit from the world. Even the text to his soon-to-be-widow was enjoyable. Finally, she knew exactly what he thought of her. Peter flipped on a hat to shield his eyes from the sun as he mused on these things.

The Skye Bridge was busy due to the tourist season being in full swing. Cars raced past him, most heading onto Skye rather away from it, but no doubt that would be reversed tonight, although he would not see it. Each was full of a family or couple. In the rear, kids would be moaning about the time taken to get there while in others, men taking their partners on a romantic day out would hope for success that night. Maybe they would be lucky and get a Sarah and not a Leah. Other cars held older people who now enjoyed watching life together, the years meaning they could not participate fully as they had. Peter would never become old. It looked horrendous.

As he reached the top of the first bridge, he saw a slight commotion on the second. Someone had stopped a car and there was a queue building behind them. The traffic out of Skye was moving normally but the red car was holding up the others. Someone was out of the car and opened the boot. Maybe it was a wheel change.

Peter ignored the issue and walked on. As long as they were clear when he got to the second bridge. He did not want an audience when he went. Slipping out, that was the way to go, like someone not noticed at a party. Who had invited him? No one knew and no one cared. Just who had brought him to his life? God? He'd be pretty pissed at his relationship with Sarah. Or would he? After all, he'd made her like that, a perfect fit for Peter. It was this world that wanted them apart.

Peter stopped briefly and took out a bar of chocolate. It was a large one, but it no longer mattered about his figure. Watching the commotion up ahead, he munched his way through the whole bar. Leah would have taken some, in fact most when he was with her. *None for you now.* Peter laughed and walked on. Up ahead, he saw the red car's wheel had been changed and it was now starting again. For this he was grateful as he was now approaching the second bridge and wanted some space to leave this world.

The cars began to break free from the long queue that had been established, and Peter found himself staring out at the sea beyond the bridge. It was beautiful, and he would miss it. Just a pity that people got in the way. Setting down his rucksack, he took out a photograph. It was Sarah on a beach in Spain. For two minutes, he simply stared before kissing the picture and then tossing it over the edge of the bridge. *Goodbye, see you somewhere better.*

It would only take a minute and Peter set his rucksack up neatly against the railings at the start of the bridge and waited for a moment, looking for a gap in the traffic. Then he noticed that red car. It was travelling past him, the opposite direction from the traffic it had held up. Bizarre, he thought, maybe it has a problem. Still, no car worries for him. Looking around he shouted 'Goodbye.'

The first thing Peter felt was a pain in his shoulder as he was blown into the railings that guarded the bridge. His ears screamed from the massive explosion that rocketed into the air. As he fell, he was sure he saw a car flip and fall over the side of the bridge. Others screamed to a halt, some crashing into each other.

In his mind, a voice screamed, *Why now? I was nearly there, so nearly.* Looking through dust, he saw a man's head up against the windscreen of his car. Blood was pouring from a cut which had been caused by the window which was now shattered. Something inside Peter stirred and he looked around desperately for his rucksack. Taking out a first aid kit, he ran towards the car and began to shout at the driver, checking if he was conscious and hoping to keep him that way.

Peter was unsteady on his feet but apart from a severe battering to his shoulders, he thought he had got away lightly from the blast, whatever had caused it. But as the dust settled, he saw that not everyone was as lucky. From being a busy conduit to the Isle of Skye, the bridge was now silent in terms of traffic but instead had become a cacophony of screams and cries of pain.

Peter opened the door of the man's car and he had to catch him as he slumped. Pushing him back into his seat, he checked the man's pulse. There was nothing. The eyes looked cold and lifeless and then from beside the man, came a scream. Peter realised that the passenger seat was also occupied but the woman there was a mass of blood and dust, her window having blown through. In the distance, he heard a single siren, police by the sound of it. They must have been close already, he reckoned and raced around the car to the woman. She was staring at the driver's seat, shouting at the man to wake up, to come to. As Peter tried to grab hold of her to calm her down, she almost attacked him, telling him to save her husband. It was too late for that and Peter saw the injuries on her chest, blood seeping from below her ribs where something was sticking into her gut. He could save her—he'd try.

A police officer ran up to Peter and yelled at him not to go any further forward on the bridge. Turning his head to look, Peter saw the road had partly fallen away, and people were being dragged away from their cars by anyone who had the strength and mobility. A piece of road suddenly slipped away, and a woman cried as she fell to the water below.

'Get the lifeboats dispatched,' shouted the policeman into his radio and then stepped forward of Peter holding out a hand for a child who was limping from a car.

'Get Dad!' shouted the child, and Peter watched the officer jump along the edge of the road surface and drag a man from the car which was close to the new edge of the road. As the constable came past Peter, he yelled at him to just grab someone and get back off the bridge. Peter nodded and fought for the woman's seatbelt. He felt her hitting him as he did so, so much in shock, she could not even understand he was saving her life.

The belt came loose at the fourth attempt and he grabbed her arm and shoulder, dragging her from the seat. Screaming, she fought with him, but he kept pulling. Normally you would not have moved her but the imminent threat of the bridge collapsing was too much to risk. And then he laughed. How was anything a risk for him? He should be dead.

Dragging the woman to where the policeman was now standing, on the road that was attached to the island in the middle of the channel, he began to try and work on her stomach, to see if he could halt the bleeding. The officer was trying to assess the man he had recovered but was constantly interrupted by the radio. Peter's hands were red as he pressed down on the wound created by a stick, made of hard plastic that had punctured the woman's stomach. What had that been doing in the front seat of the car? He would never know but he did know she was beginning to lose consciousness.

And yet, there was now a calm to the scene. Not in the sense of noise, for the cries of the wounded and of people assisting were still very much polluting the bright morning. But the dust was beginning to settle, and Peter could see the full effect of the devastation caused by what he considered must have been a bomb. After all, there was nothing else on the bridge.

But the real calmness was in Peter. He understood this pain and suffering caused by someone else. And he knew his role in it. As he worked on the woman beneath him, another part of him saw Sarah watching. She was always so amazed at his work. Flipping his head up and seeing the blue water running beyond the bridge, he realised her picture was still floating away down there. *Not yet*, he thought, *I'm needed right now. Job to do.*

Chapter 5

Macleod had stared in disbelief when he saw the pictures on the television. The bridge was so iconic in the passage over to Skye and he had driven over it recently with Jane and Hazel Mackintosh on a weekend off. Jane had loved the view from the bridge and had made Macleod walk back along it so she could stand there and simply look out into the water. She was like that with views. Jane could never glimpse something; she had to stand and suck in all the smells and listen to every sound, combining it with the visual feast before her to imprint a place on her mind. It was this sensitivity that got hold of his heart as much as her figure attracted his more basic instincts.

Parry had raced into the office, a mobile to his ear, and told Macleod he was on his way up to Skye and Macleod advised he would follow him up. Calling his superior, Macleod found that another DI was being dispatched to the scene but that he was requested to attend to help assess if the two events were connected. After calling a meeting with Hope, he left her in charge and departed Fort William in a car with Ross. Jona Nakamura grabbed him just before he left, and he advised that he would get all forensic discovery sent to her for possible connections.

'Do they know how many are dead, sir?' asked Ross as he drove past Invergarry Castle before cutting across country towards the Skye Bridge.

'There are some in the water, Ross. Coastguard are searching and the reports from the scene are sketchy at the moment. But I guess there will be a clearer picture by the time we get there. The boss said part of the bridge has given way and cars fell into the water. Total mess apparently.'

'It seems a bit much to go from a high-powered rifle shooting to a bomb at the roadside. Could be something quite different.'

Macleod shook his head. 'How often do you get a terrorist attack in the Highlands, Ross? Have we just hit the proverbial two buses coming at once? I don't think so. More likely, there's a connection but I'm just theorising. We'll see when we get there.'

'Did you see Stewart at the Fort William scene?' asked Ross but then held up his hand. 'Of course, you wouldn't have. You were probably busy.'

'Why? What was wrong?'

'When she started going about to interview and investigate, there was a nervousness, a real edge in her.'

'She's bound to feel a bit off after that attack when she nearly died, Ross.'

'I should have been there, stopped her, defended her, sir.'

'No, you shouldn't. You were fighting to save a man's life. It was the right call. She should have been more circumspect if anything. Waited for back-up. Anyway, she'll get over it.'

'I'm not sure she is. I'd keep an eye if I were you, sir.'

Ross was rarely impertinent enough to suggest a course of action to his boss and Macleod took the man's concern on board. It was strange when you thought about it. Macleod would put money down on Stewart, if he believed in gambling, money that would say she could put both him and Ross down in a fight. Maybe even the two of them at once. Yet her mind was attacking her now in a way that must be unsettling.

The roads around Skye were gridlocked and they met many traffic police trying to sort out the myriad of gawking tourists and locals, concerned relatives, journalists and cameramen, and actual police who had been sent to the incident. The force had been despatched from all parts; the local division being overwhelmed. Although they got close to the bridge, Ross had to park the car a mile away and they walked the rest of the way.

Arriving at the scene, Macleod flashed his warrant card and asked for DCI Marjorie Dalwhinnie, not his direct boss but the DCI from division who had been sent over to coordinate the incident. Advised that she would be at least half an hour, Macleod took Ross forward to as close a point to the scene as they could get that was safe and not being worked on by forensics.

Several boats were making their way back and forth about the bridge, probably in a search pattern and there was a Coastguard helicopter flying above. It seemed people were still missing in the water. Ross pointed out the orange rigid hulled inflatable boat, or RHIB, that belonged to the RNLI, the Royal National Lifeboat Institution, and then a larger vessel. No boat was crossing under the bridge at this point and Macleod wondered if they would have to route under the second crossing. Logistically, the place was a nightmare.

There were a number of cars carelessly scattered across the road ahead and Macleod saw that a few had windows blown in and even rips in their shells. It must have been a reasonable explosion. As he peered further forward, he was able to see where the bridge had fallen away and his heart sank. The sound of a blast and then to tumble into water trapped in a car; it must have been horrific.

'Macleod! Come this way, Inspector.' Turning around, Macleod saw Parry waving him over and pointing to a mobile incident room further back along the road. With Ross in tow, he marched back passing various uniformed colleagues and knocked on the door of the incident room and entered.

'Seoras Macleod. How the devil are you, Inspector? I guess you got the easy one.'

Marjorie Dalwhinnie was a tall and thin woman who reminded Macleod of a giraffe in that she could glide about a room but in a most gangly fashion. She almost had too many limbs, it seemed, and that, with her manly voice, had made her the butt of many jokes on the force. Macleod had suffered for his faith from the same teasing crowd and the pair had formed a mutual alliance, occasionally tapping into each other when they needed a boost.

'Detective Chief Inspector.'

'At least call me Dalwhinnie, you auld stickler. Good to see you, Seoras.' Macleod was enveloped in a brief hug which caught him momentarily unawares and he simply received it like she was an embracing older auntie embarrassing a young boy.

'I guess you have your hands full, Marjorie,' he conceded. 'How can I help?'

'It's going to be a while before we can pull everything together. We believe that a car, routing onto the island, stopped on the bridge and changed a wheel. At this point they also left a package under the car on the road. From the CCTV, it was like a chip wrapper, a load of newspaper and that, wrapped together but the newer stuff that they can use these days. Looked just like rubbish.'

'How big?' asked Macleod.

'That's it, it was large, good half metre square but also quite low. Easy to be driven over. The car left, drove to the roundabout over the second bridge and came back past the rubbish it left and then the bomb explodes, maybe a minute later.'

'Did you get footage of who was in the car? Licence plate.'

Dalwhinnie sighed. 'The car is burnt out, in Badicaul.'

'That's just to the north. So, they must be on foot, or have an accomplice.'

'I want you to look at the footage, Seoras, see if you recognise anyone on it from your job at Fort William, see if there's any similarities. I find it hard to believe it's not the same person, or group at least. We don't do terrorism in the Highlands—it's crazy.'

'My thoughts exactly, Chief Inspector.'

'I've got a lot to get through, but you have my number so if you think of anything, just let me know. The main incident room is set up in Kyle in a community hall there. They know you're coming.'

Macleod nodded and left the mobile incident room for the car, Ross tagging behind.

'How do you know the DCI, sir?'

'Old friend on the force. Good officer, Ross. I doubt she'll miss much here.'

It took an hour to get to Kyle, park, and arrive at the incident hall. Macleod was treated with politeness, but the place was so busy he ended up sending Ross in search of coffee while he was placed in front of a computer with a young officer. When Ross returned with the drinks, Macleod was already watching the incident.

A red car pulled up on the road and a woman got out. Macleod struggled to see well because of the distance but the woman was wearing a red dress and showing a lot of cleavage. In fact, Macleod thought she almost turned to the camera and flaunted it, a most unusual thing to do if you have pulled over with a puncture. As the incident rolled on, Macleod saw someone try to get out of their car to help but they were sent back with a firm wave of the hand and even shouted at from what he could see on the screen. There was no sound so the words were unknown, but it did look like a rebuke.

When the woman brought the tyre round to change, Macleod saw a package being removed from within the rim. The package was slid under the car when the wheel was changed and was left sitting there as the vehicle departed. The car was seen again briefly as it passed by in the opposite direction and then the feed simply stopped from the camera.

'Thoughts, Ross?'

'Very random, sir. Unlikely to know your target was going to be there. Very indiscriminate too. Does look more like terrorism than a targeted killing in disguise.'

'And any comparison with our killing back at the staircase?'

'Well, it's not the same person. I mean with our person, we do not know whether it was a man or woman, but that's a woman, sir. Even someone of my persuasion recognises a flaunted pair of boobs when I see them. She's really making sure she's got them on camera.'

Macleod sat back in his chair and pondered on this. She really was, wasn't she? It was not that these types of women did not exist outside of certain male imaginations but to show yourself to a camera in this fashion as you planted a bomb was pretty daring.

'Blow up an image of her and get it down to Nakamura along with the film. Let's rerun the film and see if we can spot anyone else from our incident. We also need to get hold of those who were close to the suspect, get a description and see what she looked like to them.' Ross nodded and Macleod watched the incident over and over again for an hour. By the end, he was no wiser than after the first run through.

Outside the hall, Macleod sucked in some fresh air and watched the sun begin to set. Being the height of summer, it would only disappear for a short while but at least it would mark the close of the day, another rough one for the Highlands. He placed a call to Dalwhinnie offering his findings and asking that he could see any interview transcripts from those who had waited around or seen the red car whose driver had planted the bomb.

'A team of police divers have pulled the car that toppled in from the depths, with four on board. We reckon two may have died before the car even fell but two look like they drowned. There'll be confirmation when the morgue gets to it. Not that it matters in the great scheme of things—they were still killed.'

'Any identification?' asked Macleod.

'All German tourists.'

'German,' interrupted Macleod. 'Our victim was German. Did you get any names?'

'Had his wallet on him. German family on holiday. We have traced the accommodation and the German authorities have informed next of kin. Franz Engel. Awaiting more details though.'

'Maybe a connection, Dalwhinnie, but I find it hard to believe they were an actual pre-determined target. The method is not robust enough.'

'I agree, Seoras but we're clutching at straws otherwise. We have nothing on the suspect. She's just vanished.'

'Okay,' said Macleod. 'I'm stopping up here tonight and then heading back down in the late morning after I get through your interview transcripts.'

'I don't mind telling you Seoras, this has been hell. The bridge being out means half my suspects are on one side with an understaffed police force. We had to call in every other service to help. It's been bedlam.'

'Any way to solve that?'

'Military engineers just turned up, going to make me a bridge and get everything flowing once we have finished with our forensics.'

'That'll be something,' said Macleod. 'I'll call in the morning when I'm off.'

Macleod called in to Hope and received a roundup of the day. Jona had finished her investigations and was currently working on the footage Macleod had sent down. Stewart was starting to look at where the weapon could have come from and if any were purchased recently.

'I'm not sure these are related closely,' said Hope, 'but it's unlikely to have two terrorist attacks in the Highlands, the first since never, and they are not related.'

'So, I keep getting told, Hope. Parry has certainly been running on the terrorist line. He's trawling groups and activity, going through their contacts in organisations. But there's still no demands, no media attention, no released videos, all incredibly quiet. It does not feel like a terrorist attack as far as

43

I can tell, but I don't have any real experience.'

Macleod dined with Ross and then excused himself to his room where he called home.

'Hello, Seoras, It's Hazel. Jane just popped out for a bottle of wine. I take it you've been busy today. Do they have you on both? Is Jona okay?'

Macleod could hear the excitement in her voice and after the time that Mackintosh had been through with her cancer treatment, he was buoyed to hear her take an interest in anything. So, he detailed out what had been happening, finding a listening ear on the other end of the line.

'If you have the video footage, let me see it,' said Mackintosh. 'Don't tell Jona though, I don't want to undercut her, just help.'

'You just want something else to do other than recover and drink wine to forget. Don't worry, I understand.'

'You don't really, Seoras.' Macleod thought of how he buried himself in work for twenty years after his first wife died. A move to Glasgow and a penchant for overtime at all times left him a bitter man who needed a change of air to bring him back to who he really was.

'I understand only too well, Hazel. I'll send it over.'

Chapter 6

Hope stretched her arms up to the headboard behind her and cursed the alarm. With a swing of the arm, she grabbed it and silenced it with her forefinger. Five in the morning was too early to be up without having someone waking you. Someone gorgeous, of course. A sudden streak of regret swept over her as she remembered it was only a few months ago she would have had Allinson reaching over. He had been good looking, but hell, he had become impossible to be with. She was glad that they had never formally moved in together, just wound up every night in one of their two bedrooms.

Throwing the covers off, Hope felt no chill as she stood up, the room being like a giant oven designed to bake whole people. That was the thing about summer when it happened up here. Generally, it was cool but when it came it came in abundance, and because your body had been used to that cooler temperature, it sweated buckets in the heat. Still, no need to complain.

Hope almost yelped when she turned on the water, even though she knew she had only allowed the cold tap to flow. The shower made sure the effect was over her whole body and she forced herself to stand in the cold, loving it, but also fighting to stop herself from shaking. It was not some large pool of reviving water that you saw in those shower gel adverts, but it was rather good.

After exiting, Hope threw on her silk dressing gown, one she had bought for Allinson but which he would no longer see. In this heat, it was ideal, and she sat at her desk, her red hair dripping slightly onto her back as she looked over various photographs of the scene of carnage at Neptune's Staircase. In a lot of ways, they had been lucky; only one dead, unlike at Skye.

There was a knock at the door and Hope heard Stewart's voice asking if she was there. Opening the door to her colleague, Hope saw that Stewart was dressed in black trousers and smart, rounded shoes. Hope was not one to force fashion on anyone else, but she would never wear such a formal looking pair. Currently she had a pair of ankle boots which also sported a low heel, allowing her to run comfortably. But that was never Stewart with her white blouse and serious glasses. Hope had to agree Macleod had done well in bringing her onto the team, even if he did seem a little too fond of the girl.

'The boss has sent down pictures of the Skye bomber, sir. I thought you'd want an early look. He's asking about whether they could be the same person. It looks unlikely.'

'Yes, he mentioned it to me last night. My goodness, look at her. Is she posing for the CCTV?'

'Bit much, isn't it? Showing off like that. You'd think it would be enough to have a body and not ...'

Hope looked up at her DC and watched her turn away. Hope stood up and placed a hand on Stewart's shoulder. 'You okay, Kirsten?'

'She was a show-off too, sir. Everything she'd got right there for him to view and adore, right before she killed him. One step from killing me.'

Hope held onto the woman's shoulder but did not know what else to do. Maybe she should embrace her, hold and support. She remembered being there for Macleod in a hotel room on Lewis and she had no hesitation in coming to his aid despite how different they were. Stewart was certainly different, but she was a woman in pain and surely Hope could reach out to her sister in the force. But something kept her aloof, a hand on the shoulder.

'Take your time; it will go. Keep doing the sessions.'

'Yes, sir,' said Stewart and walked to the door. 'I'll see you at breakfast.' As the door closed, Hope felt useless. Something had stopped her from fully warming to Stewart and she did not know what. Maybe it was because Macleod rated her so highly. Inside, she knew there was a flame for Macleod, one of those torches you do not want to acknowledge but which burns bright in your depths. But she had better start the day or he would be back and complaining about what had not been done.

Macleod entered the temporary Skye incident room and walked through the melee to the computer desk at the rear of the hall almost unnoticed. Here he was no one, really. Just a DI popping in to see if there was a link to his own case. Maybe this incident was more spectacular with part of the bridge disappearing and more dead. Parry had a full team up and they had sent a DCI to oversee the running of the case and to sit over him in regard to the Fort William incident.

Ross was already at the desk and gave his boss a nod on arrival. A coffee was sitting in a cup ready for him and Macleod thought how his team understood the little things that kept him happy. 'Thank you, Ross,' said Macleod and sat down. Beside him, Ross pulled up a chair and started to work the mouse, preparing footage from the blast.

Ross got a raw deal, really, thought Macleod. Everything he had earned in Macleod's respect had come from his hard work. Hope had a head start from how she looked. It was a bias and one he sought to eliminate but it was one that would always be there. A smiling face of a woman always picked him up, be it Hope, Stewart, Hazel, or especially Jane. He was a man after all. But then again so was Ross. Maybe he feels the same about my own smiling face, not that I smile that often. Macleod grabbed his coffee, drunk a large draught, and settled his mind from its loose wanderings to begin to focus on the task in hand.

Two hours later Macleod's head was swimming. They had scanned car after car and found nothing. No connection to their case and no one looking out of place. There were tourists, people on their way to work, truck drivers, and many more people going through the daily routine. The only person sticking out was the bomber herself. And every time Macleod saw her, he was struggling.

'Ross, let's take a break.'

'Great,' said Ross, a little too quickly, 'Shall I get you another coffee?'

'No, a proper break. Let's go out and get one and have a sit down and think. I'll get them. You get an update about any new developments and I'll see you down by the harbour.'

The air outside was stifling but at least it was less claustrophobic than the hall and Macleod made his way to the coffee shop and ordered two lattes to go. As he paid, a message came in on his mobile and he saw a picture of his partner in her dressing gown from that morning, sitting on their patio looking out to the Moray Firth. And there was that lift he had thought about. She was simply in a large dressing gown, covered from head to foot and looking like she had barely awoken, but it mattered not to him.

Ross met him at the harbour and gratefully took his coffee as they took shelter from the sun against a harbour wall. Jackets off, the two men looked the picture of the working man in summer and Macleod prayed for a breeze to make the shade even more palatable.

'German tourists in the car, sir. A train driver and the trip was planned over a year ago. Apparently, there's nothing in his background that makes him a target for anyone. But they are still digging. Mr Parry and his team are starting to take over, pushing for terrorist links but there's little forthcoming, even from whomever they have deep undercover.'

'What about the rest of the dead? Are they all identified?' asked Macleod.

'Yes, and nothing there. Eight dead in total, another twenty injured, two seriously. Four Germans died in the car that fell into the water. Another two people fell into the water and died. An English female, schoolteacher and a walker, aged seventy-five, a gentleman from Aviemore. Two more died at the scene in their cars.'

'Any more on the bomber?'

'No. A very distinct no when I asked. Gone to ground and the heat's coming down from above to DCI Dalwhinnie—at least that's the rumour. Might be some coming our way soon, sir. Although they are not saying the incidents are the same person, not even saying the same group.'

Macleod nodded and watched the sea before him shimmer

in the sun. He had been on Skye before and looked at the same stretch of water this side of the bridge and seen it churn. But it was always the same water beneath, even if the top looked different.

'Can we get a height on the bomber and our shooter? Check their frame?'

'Yes, sir, but in terms of frame, one had a rather generous bosom and the other none of note.'

'I am aware of that, Ross, but see if the height matches. Get Jona onto the footage and see if she can dig anything up. Tell her my direct request because she'll be up to her eyeballs, but I want this done and quick. I'll talk to her about it when we get back this evening. We need to trace the gun, too, or at least some possibilities.'

Macleod went silent and then stood up before walking over the edge of the harbour to stare at the sea beyond. Ross followed, coffee in hand, aware that they looked a little ridiculous in their shirt and trousers, examining the sea like a pair of tourists.

'It always changes, Ross; do you see that?'

'Yes, sir,' but Ross was struggling to see where this was going.

'How easy is it to get a pair of fake boobs? I mean, do they come custom made or do you buy them off a shelf? How convincing are they?'

'Sir?'

'Just a theory, Ross, just a theory. You see the sea is always the same underneath, just the top changes.'

'Well, the tides and currents change, sir.'

'Don't bust your boss' analogy, Ross; let him have his moment.'

'Sir!'

The rest of the morning was spent checking the footage one last time and Macleod wondered if he could actually see anything clearly by the end of it. His eyes were swimming when he got a text from DCI Dalwhinnie summoning him to her office at the rear of the hall he was working in.

The Inspector was behind her desk, which was a sea of papers and photographs, and in her hand was a cigarette. Behind her, a window was open and she turned away from it as Macleod entered.

'Thank God, Seoras, a friendly face.' She smiled and then put her spare hand to her mouth. 'Sorry, I shouldn't blaspheme before you. It's just a bit hectic.'

Macleod saw bags under the woman's eyes and wondered if she had managed any sleep since this incident had started. Probably not if she was as conscientious as she had always been. He watched her take a draw on her cigarette and then flick the ash out of the window.

'Excuse the cancer stick, but it's been rough. I have the big chiefs on every hour, Parry with his theories at me, and to top it all, a suspect I have nothing on. We're looking at a lucky DNA find or something akin to that. Or else someone coming forward to identify our bomber. Hell, Seoras, we have next to nothing.'

'Has Parry not got anything from his sources?'

'Nothing. Oh, he covers it with intel about this and that, but he has nothing that directly relates to this. They are all screaming terrorist but who the fuck blows up the Skye Bridge, Seoras—who?'

Macleod dropped his head.

'Sorry, shouldn't have sworn in front of you either. I need you to find your shooter, Macleod. They are saying now it's

51

an unrelated incident, just a wild gunman, but I am not sure.'

'Me neither, sir. I also am not sure your bomber is a she, but I don't have the proof.' Dalwhinnie raised her eyebrows but then seemed too preoccupied to think about the implications.

'Get back to Fort William, Seoras, and work through your investigation. Any help on this, run through me directly; I'll keep you in the loop. But from on high, you are on a separate case, you got that. But keep in touch, daily. You have my number, my direct number.'

Before setting off for Fort William, Macleod took a moment to ring home and ended up spending over half an hour on his mobile. Jane had been up through the night with Hazel who had been extremely depressed. Through yawns, his partner detailed how their guest seemed to be unable to focus on anything but her own condition. Her hair loss was upsetting her, the loss of her buxom figure leading to deep contemplation on why she had deserved this and at the heart of it all was a deep loneliness.

'You know I can't come back at the moment,' said Macleod.

'I do and that's why I haven't asked you to, love. But I need to get her active, take her mind away from her suffering, from what she's lost.'

'It's bound to affect you. Is she seeing the councillor yet?'

'Refuses,' said Jane. 'Doesn't want no damn shrink in her head. Probably more frightened to face up to what has happened.'

'From what I know of her she'll face that bit. I think she's seen just how alone she is. She's fortunate you're there.'

'I'm not sure I want to be, Seoras. Do you have anything you can give her to look at, to take her mind away from it?'

'I'll need to talk to Jona. I can't just fire stuff out without her knowing, or agreeing. And Hazel will have to keep anything I give to her quiet. But she'll know that. I'll see what I can do.'

'Good,' Jane said and then went silent for a moment. 'Be as quick as you can. We could do with some 'us' time. Hazel's not the only lonely one.'

Sitting beside Ross as they drove back to Fort William, Macleod thought over the overnight bag that was stowed in the house until an emergency called for his departure. He had moved in with Jane for a reason, to share a life and yet he seemed to be dragged away more and more for investigations. Maybe it was time to think about getting out. He could go for a consultancy somewhere. They were all getting younger around him anyway and it was not as if he lacked savings. A wee bit of moonlighting here and there would see him comfortable, and in a position to give more time to Jane, and to himself.

'You okay, sir?' asked Ross as they drove along the side of Loch Lochy.

'Yes, why?'

'You haven't said a lot since we left Skye, sir. And if I may say, you seem to be fretting a little.'

'Fretting? No, not fretting—maybe pondering.'

'On that bomber.'

Macleod actually laughed before he could stop himself. 'No, Ross, something quite different. Tell me how long are you going to stay in this game? It must take you away from David a lot.'

'Well, he's not at the flat that often in truth. He's busy trying to promote his art, so I have quite a few nights alone. But it's for a time, we both know that, until he can get settled, have better contacts, then he'll travel less.'

'Don't make it too long; you get tired of being alone. There's nothing like a good woman to come home too. Sometimes you don't want to leave.'

Ross gripped the steering wheel uncomfortably. 'If I may say so, you're becoming more philosophical these days, sir.'

'Don't tell the girls, Ross. I'm just thinking things over.'

'That's usually the start of it.' Looking straight ahead, Ross left the comment hanging.

'Becoming a philosopher yourself, Ross.' Macleod looked out at the expanse of water they drove beside and saw a motor cruiser in the sunshine. On the aft deck, a woman of maybe fifty sat with her legs up and a cocktail of some variety in her hand. Across from her, a man in a panama hat was talking to her with a beer in his hand. No one was near them, the nearest boat being much further down the loch. *That looks like something worth starting*, thought Macleod.

Chapter 7

Sitting in the community hall office, Macleod listened as Hope gave the last part of her debrief to him. They were almost done with the forensics in the area. The car the shooter had used had been picked over, or what remained of it after being burnt out, but there was nothing gained from the hours of painstaking work. Stewart was pushing some leads, looking for the weapon and where it may have been bought but again there was nothing.

Hope indicated a file on the cloud server they used where Macleod could find all the witness statements along with the cross referencing that showed they were clearly looking for someone in a hood. Whether that person was a man or woman, no one could tell for sure.

'So, in short, during my absence, we haven't gone forward at all,' said Macleod.

'There have been no new leads to follow. But it's not like we haven't been looking.'

'Sorry, Hope, been a long day. There's a good DCI up in Skye getting the run around and I would love to help her out. She's a good one.' He stood up and walked to the door of the office. 'I'm seeing Miss Nakamura later on, a personal favour to me. Hazel Mackintosh is struggling, Hope, and I want to give her some things to occupy her mind. It's not a slur on Jona who's doing great in the circumstances, but another pair of eyes won't hurt and it'll pick the woman up. Just so you know why I'm letting Mackintosh in.'

He turned back to Hope and saw her shoulders flopping against the back of the chair. Part of him thought she could do with someone getting a hold of those shoulders and massaging them, forcing out all the concerns of the day. But as her boss, that might not be construed in the correct manner, if indeed it was only concern prompting him.

'Get to bed and get some rest, Hope. You looked shattered. Tomorrow we'll look at a different point of attack on this.'

'What point?' asked Hope, shoulders lifting and an eagerness in her voice.

'I don't know, that's what tomorrow is for. Go sleep!'

Macleod checked his watch as Hope departed and saw that he had two hours to kill until he was meeting Jona. The time was already nine o'clock and although the daylight was not gone, he was feeling tired like Hope. But Jona was looking to complete something so she had not been able to meet until eleven unless urgent, so he would have to wait. But if he got the okay tonight, then he would have something to occupy Hazel if she had a restless night. *If? More like when.*

Stepping outside the community hall that served as the temporary base, Macleod walked the short distance to Neptune's Staircase. It was still cordoned off and would be opened tomorrow. At this time, there were only a few uniforms guarding the scene until forensics gave the all clear for reopening and Macleod was able to wander along the path on his own.

The person would have to buy the weapon and maybe not

too far in advance given his ability at handling it—or maybe it was *her* ability. It had been an upward shot to a balcony with a guard rail in front of it, so that the person needed to hit the torso or head. If the shooter were in a hideout, the shot would have been easy, all the time in the world to simply line it up before firing, hidden from the world. But this was in the open. Why?

Holding the rifle would be more awkward, too. Quick up to the shoulder and you'd have to take the kick. A trained soldier would have no problems but then they would have shot straighter. Again, his thoughts came to the weapon.

Maybe it's a new buy, a first timer. Stewart's not getting a bite trawling around the usual contacts but there are guys who would not say anything, deep in the black market. We would never get near them. Maybe the shooter does their homework even if they can't shoot. Maybe a seller is panicking, thinking this might come back on him, especially if the buyer was a newbie.

Macleod took out his mobile and searched for a number he did not like to call but had proved useful in the past. He knew it would come with a cost, a quid pro quo at some point but he needed this deadlock broken.

'Smythe, it's Macleod, where are you at present?'

'Well, good evening, Inspector; always good to hear your voice, and concerned about my welfare. No need to worry—I'm perfectly safe where I am.'

Macleod forced himself to not get annoyed at the Ulsterman's banter. Patrick Smythe was a private investigator working the west coast of Scotland based out of Stranraer, but he had helped Macleod before, asking for certain information in return. A former member of the police in Ulster, he retired after a bomb blast took his arm off. Now he worked privately but he had deep connections into the underworld and operated on a shadowy line, sometimes in not the most legal of ways.

'You heard about the shooting in Fort William?' asked Macleod.

'I heard the gunfire, Macleod. I'm in Corpach on Craigantlet with Maggie, enjoying the sun. I take it you're on the case and this is no social call. Meet me in half an hour. Loch Linnhe pier. And bring some tea. Maybe a donut, or a wee pastry, Macleod.'

Hanging up the call, Macleod fought to control the anger. *Cup of tea and a donut. Cheeky rascal.* Realising there was nothing much he could do before needing to depart for his rendezvous with Smythe, Macleod advised the officer on watch at the hall that he was going out for an hour and that he would be available on his mobile. Taking the pool car, Macleod drove into Fort William stopping at a petrol station, one with a small supermarket and bought tea and coffee and a donut. Finding a car park along from the pier, Macleod then strolled to the gates that blocked entrance further onto the pier.

'Detective Inspector, you are more than punctual,' said a voice with that blunt Belfast tone. 'And I see you've brought me a wee cuppa too. Is that a donut? That's cracking—you must be in dire need of my services.'

Macleod spun around to see a single-armed man in a t-shirt and jeans, with a baseball cap on his head. The sun, although not fully set for the night, was certainly low enough to make the cap redundant and Macleod wondered if the man was trying for a younger look.

'Tea! Donut!' said Macleod handing over the items as if he was paying for entry into a museum. 'Now listen up and no wise cracks. I haven't a lot of time.'

'Need to get back to see that DS of yours—McGrath, isn't it? Or do you need to catch up with Ross or Stewart?'

'So, you know my team, not exactly difficult. But I wonder if you know a lot more people on the darker side?'

'If you didn't think so, Macleod, you wouldn't be here. So, what's the trouble for you? Someone told me you guys have nothing on the incident here or up in Skye.'

Macleod kept a restrained face. The man always seemed to know more than he should. 'I need to trace the gun that was used up here. We're going through the usual channels but drawing a blank. We've got nothing on it except a picture.'

Macleod handed over what was a blurred shot of the hooded gunman and the weapon. Smythe took the photo after setting down his tea and studied it carefully. The man stood with his back to the dying sun, so Macleod had to squint into it. As he looked up, Macleod saw a smirk.

'Sorry Inspector, a force of habit. Always have them squinting at you. Any idea where I'm looking for the gun?'

Macleod tilted his head slightly. 'I reckon it might be local, as in Glasgow or Edinburgh, but given that we haven't traced a seller yet or heard of anyone, it might be one of the better black-market sellers. The shooter struggled to handle it so you might want to look for an over-the-odds sale to an unknown. You have better links into that world than we do, Smythe.'

'Better than a Glasgow detective? I'll get on to it for you. How quick do you want an answer?'

'I'd take one right now.'

'I'll ring you tomorrow with something,' said Smythe, picking up his tea and securing the donut in the same hand. Macleod watched as the man bent down to bite into the donut and then slurp some tea as he straightened. It looked so awkward but Smythe did it as if these were the most normal actions.

As he turned to walk away, Smythe stopped and turned round, a rather serious look on his face. 'Not that I'm unappreciative, Macleod but you see when you buy someone a wee bite and a drink because you want them to help you, don't pick it up from the nearest garage. Do a wee bit of research and get something good. The donut's passable but frankly, this tea's pish.'

'Just get me something.'

Watching Smythe walk off, Macleod struggled to know how to feel about the man. He always felt the Ulsterman was playing him, but he knew he got results. Maybe not always the result a serving officer could allow but always a result.

Returning to the car, Macleod felt his mobile vibrate in his pocket and answered it. 'Sir,' he said realising that the number was that of DCI Dalwhinnie.

'Seoras, just a quick update for you. The bomb up here was comprised of Semtex that has been traced to a batch that was also responsible for explosions in Northern Ireland carried out by the dissidents that are still active. A couple of smaller explosions two years ago but nothing that was lethal or on this scale. But the Irish connection might help focus your search for your man or woman. I'll get the detail emailed through for you. Anything new to report on your end?'

Macleod updated the DCI on his thoughts about the weapon and that they were searching out weapons' dealers, but he did not mention Smythe. Going to the man was something he had only learnt recently after Smythe had helped him in a murder case. Macleod was certainly not about to advertise this extracurricular source.

After hanging up the call, Macleod drunk the rest of his coffee in the car, watching the sun set. Smythe had been correct; the coffee was far from good, maybe even 'pish' as the Ulsterman had called it and Macleod tossed the cup into a bin with over a third of the liquid remaining.

When he arrived back at the temporary operations hall, Macleod saw Jona Nakamura just exiting her car and he rolled down the window, calling her over. The diminutive Asian sported a pair of black jeans and a blouse with her black hair tied up behind her.

'Your office, sir?'

'No, Jona. Can you get into the car and we'll go for a drive? It's something personal I need to talk to you about and I don't want any prying eyes or listening ears.'

The woman almost balked at first but then circled the car and opened the passenger door, climbing in. They sat in silence as Macleod drove off and he headed towards Corpach where the Caledonian Canal comes out into Loch Linnhe. As they arrived Macleod saw a number of yachts and other vessels tied up, awaiting the reopening of the Staircase and Macleod indicated that they should walk. Crossing over the canal, he found a bench looking out into the Loch and Jona sat down beside him.

'Sorry to drag you out here but I really wanted to have this discussion away from the team, both yours and mine. It's of a personal nature and … ' Macleod saw the woman's eyes widen and he suddenly realised what she must be thinking. 'No, I'm a married man, Jona, well in a partnership. It's not about me, it's about Hazel.'

'What about her?' asked Jona.

'How much do you know about why she's not here?'

'She told me in a long call one night. About the cancer and how she had been operated on. Said they had removed the cancer but had also removed … ' Jona's face was sullen and Macleod thought he saw tears in the woman's eyes. 'She spent a lot of time talking about that to me. I wasn't really ready for it, sir.'

'Seoras, please. This is personal business, not police, so please, I'm just Seoras now. She's staying at my place, and Jane, my partner, is helping Hazel—along with myself. But she's becoming more and more morbid, Jona. I was wondering if you would be all right if I fed her some of the forensic work to look at. Not to second guess you or correct anything, I have full trust in you; you need to understand that. It's just to give Hazel something to think about other than herself. Would you be okay with that? I know you are up to your eyeballs at the moment. And you'll have the other parts of the process calling in from Skye and Parry's mob.'

Jona turned on the bench, sliding a knee up so she could sit facing Macleod. The woman was smiling, almost laughing. 'Do you know, she said to me you're a sweetie underneath? Her very words. When I first met you, I was pretty intimidated, but Hazel said no, that I was misjudging you. She talked a lot about you. It's no wonder she's turned to you; she has no one else, sir.'

'Seoras, Jona.'

'Of course, it's okay, I'll be available if she wants to discuss anything. Hazel's the best and she can look over my work anytime. You are a heck of a man for helping her like this. You and your partner. But one thing. It's going to be sir, not Seoras. I don't think I could see you as anything but the boss.'

62

Macleod smiled. 'I'm not too sure how to take that, Jona, but thanks for this. Hazel really needs it. You really are an impressive young woman.'

Jona burst out into a fit of laughter before controlling herself causing Macleod to wonder what he had said. 'Sorry, sir, it's … oh, it's nothing.'

'What? Tell me what? You can't simply laugh like that and say nothing.'

'Well, it's just something Hazel said. She reckoned that if an older guy tells a young woman that she's really impressive what he means is he really likes the look of her but he realises there's too many years between them to ever have a hope in hell of making it work.'

Macleod reddened. Of course, there was an element of truth in it, but Mackintosh was outrageous. He turned to Jona. 'If you think I'm going to answer that, you're sadly mistaken. Come on, let's get you back.'

'Wait,' said Jona. 'Do you mind if we just sit here a minute? Or you can leave me here and I'll get a taxi.'

'Are you okay?'

'Yes, sir. It's just it's been hectic these last days and I'm now finally at a point where I'm at least on top of things if not fully in control. I've been looking at bodies and destruction both here and on footage from Skye. And now you bring me here, I mean, look at that view down the loch. I just want to take a moment, just want to soak in the goodness.'

Macleod regarded the woman and forcibly stopped himself using the word impressive. But she was. And not in the shallow sense of simply sweet to look at. Hope had mentioned that Jona was somewhat deeper than herself, more connected with life itself. Like Macleod, Jona was managing a team, rarely alone, and had a lot of pressure on her. And she had found an oasis. Maybe he should join her.

'Not a moment, Jona; let's take at least a half hour. You can teach me to soak this all in properly.'

Jona turned and simply stared off into the distance. Macleod regarded her and then did the same. He found himself fidgeting and a hand slapped his thigh. 'Sorry, sir, but just stop. Listen, breathe but for goodness sake, just stop.'

'Okay, but you might have to teach me how.'

Chapter 8

Hope rolled over in the bed and nearly swore at the wall she now faced. What was it with hotels and their air conditioning? It was either freezing or they had you living in a sauna. The cold would have been manageable as she could always add pyjamas and then a jumper. Maybe even blankets or an extra duvet though she had never needed any before. But the heat was unmanageable. Hope hated the duvet and often just slept under a sheet but even that was too much now, and she threw it back hoping for a blast of cool air across her skin. She was disappointed.

Her mobile vibrated and Hope rolled back over to the small side table, grabbing the device like it was about to vanish.

'McGrath! Oh, it's you, Seoras. They've traced Semtex? Okay, I'll be with you in ten minutes.'

Hope hauled herself up from the bed and half stumbled into the bathroom where she threw back the shower curtain and looked at the thermostatic control for the shower. The lack of sleep over the last three hours meant she was looking with bleary eyes and could not focus fully on the numbers. Still, she could see the blue markings and flicked the device in that direction. Stepping into the shower, the cold water felt invasive but good, like a noisy friend hauling you from your bed. After three minutes, it became simply cold and Hope stepped out grabbing a towel. Time to work.

Macleod met her and the rest of his senior team at the community hall near Fort William where he gave a quick brief. It seemed that Semtex had been used in the Skye Bridge bombing and when the forensics had consulted with their colleagues from the Garda in the south of Ireland, they had come up with a match. But it was a match from ten years ago and had been used by a Seamus Finney. He had been caught merely in possession of the bomb-making substance, not in the prosecution of making any devices and so having served a small sentence had moved to the South of Scotland. It was said he had reneged on any links with Republican groups, but he was on a watch list. The last address for the man was Fort William.

'And so,' said Macleod, 'we need to pick him up. He's not thought to be overly dangerous but be careful. That's why they want us to do it rather than the uniforms. Parry from the terrorist squad will be coming down presently from Skye but he did not want to wait to apprehend Finney, so we're to grab him.'

'Where's the address, sir?' asked Hope.

'It's a farm out towards Ben Nevis so be aware he has plenty of scope to run even if we close off the road. There's only the one road passing by the farm, but he may have plenty of places to hide things, including himself.'

'Who are you taking with you, sir, and how do you want to play it?'

'I don't—it's your operation, McGrath. I need Stewart for something here, so take Ross and whatever uniform you need and bring the man back real soon. I don't want to keep Mr

Parry waiting when he arrives. I'm afraid these incidents are growing well beyond us so we may find ourselves getting sidelined. So, let's make sure we do it right before we are put on the bench!'

'Sir,' said Hope, and nodded at Ross to indicate she would meet him outside. The man followed and once outside Hope asked him to round up about six uniforms and cars to join them and advised she would brief them in ten minutes. While she waited, Hope also spoke to Jona Nakamura, advising her to have someone on standby as any discoveries would need a thorough going over from the forensic team.

Within half an hour, and with the sun beginning to streak round Ben Nevis, the team drove out to the farm given as Finney's last address. Hope studied a photograph of the man as Ross drove along. The man was smaller than Hope, standing only five feet six and had wispy blonde hair, his crown going decidedly bald. He seemed bony and his chin was jutting out, indicating a possible broken jaw at some point.

The farm was nestled in the shadow of Ben Nevis, Scotland's largest mountain and already that colossus had tourists crawling around its lower car parks as well as many starting to climb. Hope did not see the attraction at this hour of the morning, but it would be preferable to being woken from a hotel sauna and cast out to search some random farm. At least it was summer and light, and there was no rain.

Ross drove through the gates of the farm which were open and tied back. They looked like they rarely moved, and a tractor sat beside the large farmhouse also seemed to have taken up residence. A small hatchback was further back and Hope saw a barn with doors open to the elements and little else inside it. Approaching the front door of the house with

Ross, she rapped the knocker and waited for a response. She nodded at the uniforms to encircle the house and for one to stand at the gate, but nothing was moving. Hope tried the door and it swung open.'

'An unlocked door, Ross,' she said. 'I think that warrants me going inside to see if the occupant is safe and well. Just in case someone got here before us.'

Hope called out to Finney and then walked into the front hall before shouting up the stairs and then down the hall through the open kitchen door. She quickly walked through the house before coming back outside and shaking her head to Ross.

'Bed was slept in, not overly warm but otherwise nothing. No phone, no breakfast dishes, or crumbs.'

'Let's get a look around the farm,' said her DC and he strode off for the barn. Hope followed but kept her circle of uniforms around the farm in case Finney broke from somewhere yet unseen. The barn was large with a mezzanine floor on which some bales of straw were stacked. The ground floor was almost entirely empty except for an old car which had its doors missing and a large spread of rust across the roof.

'I'll check the mezzanine, Ross—see what you can find around the ground floor,' said Hope and raced up the ladder that led to the upper floor. Squeezing between bales of hay, Hope searched the area thoroughly but came up with nothing, no hidey-holes or crevices the wanted man could be found in. On descending, Ross advised he had found nothing either and Hope stared at the car.

'Macleod had a car covering a hide in the floor when we were in Harris. Let's shift the car and see if we can find anything.'

Ross let off the car's handbrake and together they pushed it off its current spot, but underneath was only more concrete floor. As they rolled the car back to its original spot, Hope heard something underneath the car fall to the ground. Ross pulled on the brake and the pair dived to the floor and looked underneath. Where the boot would be a panel had fallen off the underside, one that was roughly cut and fashioned. Ross gingerly reached up into the void it left and then brought his hands out quickly, sliding out from under the car.

'Look,' he said holding up his hand for Hope to examine. 'Red like plastic, malleable. Looks like there was a space for storing in the car. I'm no expert but I thought Semtex was a red plastic.'

'Certainly seems suspicious. And it's also empty so I wonder if he's grabbed whatever is there and legged it. Let's scan the surroundings, see if anyone's made a move.'

Outside the barn, the pair of detectives began to search the perimeter and found several paths that led to the wooded area behind the farm. Calling over a few uniform officers, Hope instructed them to walk along the paths and to advise if they saw anything. Meanwhile, she walked a central path into the woods with a female officer while Ross held his position at the farm to make a call for Jona to come with her forensic team to examine the discovered plastic.

The path into the wood was cut well for about thirty metres but then abruptly stopped but Hope could see what would be deemed a sheep track, a thin strip of well-worn track that was naturally worn rather than man-made. As she crept along into the woods, she found herself having to duck and dive below stray branches as the ground turned to the dark grey of fallen tree debris.

Just as she was considering returning, she saw something move up ahead. Slowly, she crept forward and came upon a spot of disturbed ground which seemed to have been swept and possibly was also cut into. Her fellow officer knelt down beside her. She did not know the woman but the younger female turned to Hope as she picked some moss from the ground.

'Looks like this was stashed back on top. I reckon there could be something under here, Ma'am.'

As Hope was going to reply, she saw a black club coming down and threw herself sideways. However, the Constable was not so fortunate and took a blow straight on the top of the head.

'Bastards!' said a voice, 'Take that, you bitch!'

Another blow came Hope's way but now prewarned, she grabbed the assailant's wrist and used his swing to assist him straight to the floor. She then roughly bent his arm back and grabbed the other flailing wrist. Within seconds, she had cuffed the man and was standing over him.

'Ross!' shouted Hope. 'Any officer, this way, please.'

It took about two minutes before the first officer arrived and Hope simply waited, her foot on the man's back. She ignored his casual swearing and instead wondered if this was Finney. She could only see the rear of his head and was not getting too close until she had back up. Her colleague lay groaning on the floor, but Hope could see no blood. One of the new arrivals assisted her.

With the man escorted to a police car, Hope called Jona telling her they had a dangerous scene and to request the help of EOD, the Explosive Ordnance Division. There was little to do except wait for the cavalry, so Hope returned to the farm and spoke to her suspect. It was definitely Finney now that she saw him upright.

'You can stay tight lipped, Finney, but they are after you for the Skye bombing so any help now would be noted.'

'It wasn't me,' said the man. 'I haven't been near that bridge. It was a half-arsed effort; I'd have brought the whole lot down. It's a fecking outrage. Just because our countries had a wee debate some time ago.'

'What about the plastic explosive in the car, Finney? They matched some of your old Semtex to the bridge.'

Hope saw the man's face drop. 'So, he used it for that. The daft bugger—that's why he didn't manage to blow up the whole bridge.' The man was shaking his head.

'What do you mean?'

'You said it. You said they traced the Semtex to me. Was it from that stash they found me with? How long ago was that? These are explosives. That stuff wouldn't have gone off, it's so long past it's sell-by it's ridiculous. Five years, ten tops with that stuff. He said I didn't have enough but I did if it was fresh. But what I sold him wouldn't have got him anywhere. He must have bulked up on it. Either that or he's used something else with it. Daft bugger. Told me he was a collector, history man.'

'Why hide it and then move it if it's useless?' asked Hope.

'Because the other stuff isn't. Stupid bugger. I needed the cash.'

'So, what are you doing with the other stuff?' The man was silent. 'Who was that for?'

'Look, love, that kind of thing gets you killed. The other bloke was a stupid customer being given dud gear. The other stuff, let's say I actually value my life. It's mine, that's all I'm saying.'

Hope turned away and saw Macleod arriving in a squad car closely followed by an ambulance for her wounded constable.

All in all, it had been a good morning's work and Macleod would be delighted. As he approached, he reached out and shook her hand.

'Fill me in and tell me we have our man.'

'Yes and no,' answered Hope and explained the situation.

'That's worrying. It's one thing having terrorists on the loose but if they are amateurs, then we are in trouble. They won't be accurate, and the general public might be more at risk. Parry's going to be here in an hour, so we'll get Finney back to Fort William to a lock up. No doubt they will move him quickly from there.'

'I still don't get it, sir,' said Hope. 'Are the two attacks linked or are they separate? They seem so different, but both seem extremely amateur.'

'My money says they are linked, Hope, but with the national heat it's bringing, we'll be out of it soon and the big cheeses from the terrorist unit will be on it. It will only be Jona Nakamura and her team and the odd uniform on this. Unless they reckon there's going to be a spate and then you'd better be ready for the overtime. Still good work, McGrath. And you too, Ross,' finished Macleod spying his other colleague.

Hope sat down on the steps of the farmhouse, watching the forensic team arrive. The key was surely the gun now. If they could trace the buyer of that and of the dud Semtex then they'd know if it was an individual or a group. But no group had spoken.

Hope's mobile went off and she saw a message from Allinson: *WATCH THE TV NEWS NOW. POLICE SAY NATIONALISTS BEHIND BOMBING.*

Chapter 9

Macleod was sitting with Parry, interviewing Finney the Irishman who had been found with bombmaking materials, when his mobile vibrated in his pocket. As he was not the one asking all the questions, he took it out and glanced at it. There was no picture associated with the incoming call but instead simply the words *The Ulsterman*. Macleod slipped his mobile back into his pocket and continued to sit and listen to the questions for another two minutes before asking Parry for a recess to use the bathroom.

'As we don't seem to be getting much conversation from Mr Finney,' said Parry, 'I guess that's a good idea. We'll take ten minutes, Macleod.'

Macleod always tried to keep his connection with Patrick Smythe a secret both as a courtesy to him as a source of information but also because Smythe sometimes blurred the lines in his activities and Macleod did not want his name associated with this sort of activity. Although he was convinced that Smythe was a decent man at heart, Macleod was a little wary of his methods.

Stepping into the toilets and to make it look like he needed the requested toilet break, Macleod then stepped outside for some fresh air and called Smythe.

'I just walked from an important interview for this Smythe, so it had better be good.'

'Hello to yourself, Macleod. And as always, I deliver,' said the Ulsterman. 'I can get you a meeting with the dealer who sold the gun that was used at Fort William, but I warn you they are nervy. And it'll need to be tonight. Can you get here?'

'Where's here?' asked Macleod.

'Your old stomping ground, Glasgow. I'll meet you at eleven at the South Rotunda off the Govan road. On foot too, please. I'll provide the transport.'

'Okay, Smythe but it won't be me. I won't be able to get out of here without looking suspicious. You'll be meeting a dark-haired colleague of mine, looks small but packs a punch. And no risks, Smythe, she's there to talk to the dealer, not get involved in anything. I take it the guy doesn't know your connections to us.'

'I'll fill her in on the back story when she gets here. One whiff that you're police and the dealer will scarper, and you'll never see them again.'

With that, the call was ended and Macleod saw Parry waving at him to re-join his interview with Finney. Holding up two fingers to indicate he required two more minutes, Macleod touched the face of Stewart on his phone.

'Stewart, Macleod. I need you to drive down to Glasgow, I have a special job for you tonight.'

The boss had been direct when he had spoken with her some three hours ago. Prior to that, Kirsten Stewart had no idea why she was in Glasgow or what she was going to do. Macleod had spoken briefly to send her here and then had been out of contact until he rang her that evening. As she walked along the Govan Road, the trees blowing gently on a warm night and the grass on the verges of the roads overgrown in the height of summer, she kept her eyes peeled in the fading light.

Approaching the Rotunda building which sat beside the offices of one of Scotland's major broadcasters, she could see the colourful lights of the bridge across the Clyde and heard a city in full swing. Soon there would be people crawling out of pubs and maybe heading on to nightclubs, but here just a little way up the river, while the traffic was still busy, the pavement had few people on it.

Stewart was dressed in black jeans and a t-shirt with a leather jacket over the top. Her hair was loose and blew out across her face in the light wind she was feeling. Macleod had suggested she wear heels *to look the part,* but Stewart was unsure exactly what part that was. Her boss had said she was going along as the sidekick to a man pretending to be from a gang who the victim at the Fort William shooting had belonged to. She got that and had already decided to use a German tinge to her voice, but the heels were too much. Stewart had never worn any in her life and now would not be the first time. She could not run in them, heck, not even stand in them at times, so she was wearing her boots.

Waiting in front of the Rotunda, Stewart tried not to look like she was a working girl looking for a pick-up, but she was aware that she did look a little out of place. A taxi pulled up in front of her and a door swung open. 'Get in,' said an Irish voice. It was a hard accent and she recognised it as being from the north of Ireland.

Stepping into the car, she saw a one-armed man who offered his only hand to her. Stewart shook it and then sat in silence as the taxi pulled away.

'Evening, Miss Stewart, or for tonight, we shall say Fraulein

Vogt. You are my sister, and my muscle for tonight's meeting so you don't need to say anything. I'll address you as Frauke if I need to. Adds a little personal touch. I'm Jonas.'

'Okay,' said Stewart, a little unsurely, 'and what's your relationship with the man we are going to see?'

'Who said it was a man? I don't know if it's a man or a woman. I have never seen the person but we will tonight. We're paying a visit as an aggrieved party due to the reckless use of the gun that was purchased. I know they are not happy with it either so we may be able to get details but be warned, this is no social visit. Oh, and the guy driving us at the moment is Hans. He's going to try and monitor what's being said and maybe get some of the dialogue, but we will not be wearing any wires. If they discovered that, we could end up in trouble. And I mean bottom-of-the-river trouble. So tonight, stay sharp and quiet and let me handle it. You got that, Frauke?'

'Ja,' said Stewart.

'Damn, that's good,' said Smythe.

The taxi drove across Glasgow and approached a warehouse on the outskirts in an industrial park. Every unit was quiet, only the occasional light keeping a watch in the now dark night. Stewart could feel her palms sweating but worked hard not to show any fear. The car pulled up to a gate where a man ran out from the dark to open it and Hans drove his vehicle up to the door of a rather bland factory unit. A small light above a door came on and the green door swung open to reveal a strapping man dressed in black. Kirsten looked at him and immediately saw him as the muscle.

As her role was being the muscle tonight, she stepped out of the car and walked around to the side that Paddy Smythe occupied. He emerged from the vehicle as Hans opened the door for him, dressed in shades and a smart suit. She had watched him in the taxi place a false arm into a sling to make it look like he was injured, and to give the appearance of two arms.

Without a word, Smythe walked past the enormous muscle man and onto the factory floor followed by Stewart. Inside, the place was lit up brightly and Stewart saw a number of silvery machines that made the place look like an oversized kitchen. As they walked into the middle of the floor, Stewart saw a small group of people at the far end where a chair had been placed. Standing before it was an older woman, dressed in a suit with two strong, youthful men beside her and a woman in an evening dress.

Smythe walked confidently towards this group and Stewart followed close behind. As they arrived at the chair, the woman in the suit held up a hand for them to stop.

'Search them,' she said, and Stewart felt a pair of hands behind her start to feel her hips and then work down a leg. The search might just have been thorough and not leery, but Stewart did not appreciate the attention. She stepped forward, away from the hands, and turned yelling in German at the man. He looked across at the woman in the suit and she nodded at him to resume.

If they search Smythe like this, thought Stewart, *they'll find his fake arm.* As the man reached forward, she slapped him away and took off her jacket whirling it round. 'Look, no weapons,' she said in her best German accent.

'Search her very thoroughly,' said the woman in the suit.

The man reached forward with hands that were ready to not simply search Stewart but that were ready to grab and hold her in an unpleasant fashion while he would give her a deep examination. Stewart decided that she needed to make sure their company kept a little distance. As the man stretched, she grabbed his arm and pulled it behind him. With her other hand, she drove him off his feet, assisted by a sweep of one leg and then followed him to the ground where she pushed his face into the hard floor. Another jerk of his arm up behind him caused the man to cry out.

'We did not come here to be treated as the enemy,' said Smythe in a terse German accent, 'just for some information.'

'And information costs, my German friend.' With that the two men behind the suited woman drew handguns. 'You show up, trail me without any prior warning or even influence. I don't know your name, so I will be careful. Strip them and check for weapons.'

'In the taxi outside,' began Smythe, 'is the handgun involved in the bank robbery on Market street Edinburgh, the one six years ago where the security guard was killed. I know of your involvement because I have traced that handgun to you. Similarly, I believe you supplied the weapon used at Fort William recently which is why I am here. Now if you continue with this nastiness, I shall be forced to let my people reveal all sorts of information about what you do, specifically your involvement in that bank robbery murder, so let's be calm and sensible. Guns away and let's talk.'

Stewart noticed that Smythe did not flinch during the whole time he was speaking whereas the woman in the suit did.

'And can I speak to the real boss?' asked Smythe. The woman in the evening dress stepped forward and shooed the woman in the suit behind her.

'Impressive, my German friend,' she said. 'What do you want?'

'A friend of ours died recently at Fort William to a lone shooter, as you say. I believe you sold that gun to him. And I want his name.'

'His name, my friend, I want it too, because that kind of behaviour is bad for business. It brings attention that I don't need. So, if you get his name, then please let me know.'

'I'm afraid that's not enough,' said Smythe. 'How did you sell it to him? You must have met. In Germany we like to see the eyes before we sell. Know that someone is competent.'

Stewart, still holding the large man by the arm, watched as the woman in the evening dress considered this. She then turned to her goons with the guns and asked them to put them away. Smythe turned to Stewart and indicated she should let go of the man in her grasp. Having done so, she stood beside Smythe and watched the woman think.

'You know, my German friend, maybe you can do me a favour. I'll tell you what I know about the buyer and when you find him, dispose of him. He dropped cash in a suitcase at the services off the M80 in Stirling. We took the cash and he picked up the item from the boot of another car parked there. He must have been around the site watching to see us pick up. He also did not want to meet. Wanted to remain incognito.'

'Anything else?' said Smythe.

'No, but do make sure he suffers for me. Make an example. And don't come back here again.'

'Frauke,' said Smythe and turned on his heel with Stewart following him. She wanted to ask could they not press for more but Smythe was disappearing fast. Once outside, they got into the taxi and Hans drove away.

'Well done, Miss Stewart, but you have one more task tonight. Ring the confidential line to the police and send them a message from Frauke detailing everything we heard about the shooter in there. Then your boss can go look into the M80 services.'

'You were very cool in there. If they had tried to search us properly, they would have found your prosthetic.'

'Yes, but I had that story up my sleeve, Miss Stewart.'

'So, you have the gun?'

'What? No! I've never seen the gun. I just did my homework. I knew they were involved. I knew from certain sources they were edgy about it being missing and I simply connected some dots and played it to them. The information about our shooter was not that valuable so she was never going to risk it. I suspect when you look at the M80 services you will find your shooter but all connections to these people will be gone. I know it looked like I had the upper hand, but she was always in control. But your take down of the muscle guy was neat.'

Hans pulled the car over at a small wasteland and Smythe jumped out of the car and changed his clothes. Leaving the previous suit in the car, he tapped the boot and watched with Stewart as Hans drove the car away.

'Where's he going?'

'Well, Miss Stewart, they might try and trace the car and me, so we'll burn the car out. And I will relinquish my other arm and resume my Ulster brogue. It's a pity because I think I could have been in *The Eagle Has Landed* with that accent. Do you have a hotel for the night?'

'No, I'm driving straight back up.'

'Good, then I suggest you make that call for your boss and then we'll get a taxi back to your car and set you on your way. By the way, what's your first name?'

'Kirsten, Mr Smythe.'

'I'm Patrick, or Paddy to my friends. If you ever get bored of police work, look me up on this number only. You seem the intelligent type and that's quite rare these days.'

Stewart beamed as she took out her mobile to call the confidential line. And then she stopped. 'It's confidential but if they wanted, they could trace it, couldn't they? I mean to my number.'

'As I said, one of the rare intelligent ones. Here.' Smythe handed over a small, black mobile. 'Pay-as-you-go, one-time only.'

'Thanks. Can I ask you something?'

'Sure,' said Smythe.'

'When they pulled the guns, you were so cool. I had a recent incident and I can't get over it. In fact, if you had not have been so cool there, I might have lost it. How do you stay that cool?'

'Make the call, Kirsten, then we'll have a chat. You'll be driving in the dark so another hour's not going to hurt.'

Chapter 10

Ross yawned and ran the footage again on the screen. He had watched the same people going back and forth for a while now and his eyes were starting to blur. Beside him, Stewart followed Ross's yawn with one of her own, not having slept since her escapades the previous night in Glasgow. The adrenalin she had felt from the incident and the glowing appraisal Mr Smythe had given had kept her going so far but she was beginning to fade. And it was only mid-afternoon.

The door of the community hall opened, and Ross turned to see his bosses arrive, neither of whom had a smile on their face.

'What do we have, Ross?' asked Macleod. 'I take it you have identified the vehicles involved?'

'Yes, sir, but they have been no help. Both of them were burnt out. Our gun sellers are good, never turning to the camera and always having their faces hidden.'

'And our buyer?' asked Hope.

'Very similar. I'm trying to see if they give anything up but so far it's been textbook from them.'

'Okay; well, I have a half hour; show me the potted highlights,' Macleod instructed.

Macleod took a seat beside Ross while Stewart and Hope looked over their shoulders as Ross first let the significant footage run at full speed. A black car pulled up and a man got out, face hidden from the camera, and entered another car. About ten minutes later, a figure from the services came to the car and opened the boot before dropping in a duffel bag and taking out a long, thin case. The figure then returned to the services from which they had come. Another ten minutes passed before a car came back and dropped off a man who drove the original car away.

'So, a classic drop,' said Macleod.

'And all cars disposed of, I take it,' said Hope.

'Burned out, sir,' said Ross. 'And now disposed of.'

'Well, the drivers of the drop-off cars are professionals and they clearly know how to hide from a camera,' said Macleod. 'But what about our shooter? It's very dark in the picture. Any way we can enhance that?'

'I can get it to the lab once we know the footage we want to look at more closely, but if you note, sir,' said Stewart, 'at no point does the shooter put a face to the camera.'

'How did the shooter get there? I know it could be a female, but for now, let's assume a man,' said Hope. 'You've showed us the sellers dropping off the gun but how did our buyer arrive at the services? He is pretty far out. Did he come by car? Did he walk? Come over fields?'

'And it's dark when he did the drop. Did the buyer stop close by? Did he walk away into the distance? Did he have a car waiting, or maybe a motorbike, or a push bike? We need to expand the search of CCTV cameras in the area. Also, McGrath, get the area canvassed; see if anyone turned up locally with a long thin case to his digs for the night.'

Macleod leaned forward on his elbows and stared at the screen. 'Bring the buyer up again—the best shot we have of him.'

Ross ran the footage and then froze the screen as the figure passed by a light. The face was hidden by a hooded top and he wore trainers and a pair of jeans. Looking at the shape of the figure, Macleod could not discern whether it was a man or a woman, or what the age was.

'The figure ties into the description we have of the shooter at the canal,' said Stewart.

'Which is such a non-descript description, forgive my English,' retorted Macleod. 'Stewart, trace everyone you can who is parked in that car park or who was at the services during the time the drop is made. See if anyone remembers this person and try and fatten out the description. We're nowhere until we can at least get a description or a forensic link. Finney's not talking, although I reckon he doesn't know anything much about his buyer.'

'That's not Parry's opinion,' said Hope.

'Well, Mr Parry can investigate the Irish connection if he wants but since when did Irish paramilitaries attack Scottish canals or the Skye bridge? In fact, when did they attack Scotland as a nation? I know Finney has a history and has close contacts with a lot of nasty people back there but it's too chaotic for paramilitaries.'

'Well, the canal might be, boss, but not the bridge,' said Ross.

'Really, Ross. They would have blown the place to pieces, not some half-arsed job when parts of the road fall into the water. Besides, Finney sold them out-of-date Semtex. It wouldn't have worked.'

Hope coughed from behind. 'It kind of did, sir. Certainly

made a bang.'

'Coffee, please, someone get some coffee.' Macleod looked at his three officers and watched McGrath, then look at her subordinates.

'I'll get it,' said Stewart and shoved her glasses up to the bridge of her nose in disgust. While Stewart was away Macleod stood up and paced the room. Seeing him like this, Hope took a seat and started watching more of the playback, in an effort to steer clear of her boss.

Stewart returned and placed four cups on the computer surface. 'Sorry, Ross, but they didn't have enough sugar I had to make your second spoonful up with a sweetener instead.'

'No problem; it doesn't taste the same but at least it makes it drinkable. It still works.'

Hope took her coffee and sipped it. 'Okay, let's get down to work then. Stewart, get onto the lab and see if the footage can be enhanced, especially where the face is closest. Ross, get hold of and review further footage from the services, inside the café and that. Also, card payments—trace everyone down. I'll get hold of uniforms and get a canvass of the surrounding area going.' Hope turned to Macleod who had not touched his coffee but was instead now staring at Ross's coffee cup. 'Anything else, sir? Or does that cover it for now?'

'At least, it makes it drinkable,' Macleod mumbled. 'Half sugar, half sweetener.'

'Sir?' queried Hope.

'Where's Jona Nakamura?' asked Macleod.

'She's in conference I believe, with Parry.'

'Blast, I'll try Hazel.'

Hope raised her eyebrows to her boss, and Macleod was not sure if it was at bypassing Jona or if it was his use of the name

Hazel in front of everyone. But he didn't care and pressed the forensic officer's face on his mobile.

'Hazel, I need you to do some calculations for me about bombs.'

Over the next ten minutes, Macleod rattled off details about the bridge explosion and then shouted at his team to get him more information which he passed down the phone to Hazel Mackintosh. Every now and again, he would simply stare at the screen in front of Ross where the image of the gun buyer was still there. After a moment of silence where he seemed to be concentrating hard, Macleod nodded frantically and then thanked Mackintosh.

'Hazel's not sure,' said Macleod and ignored the looks of confusion at the use of her first name. 'But she reckons that given what we know, the hypothesis that they were going to blow up the whole bridge and not simply a part of it is a good one, given that the Semtex was old and would have probably failed to a large degree. So, they had an initial supply and then probably bought extra off Finney.'

'So why is Finney so quiet?' asked Hope.

'Because he doesn't own that explosive, he's keeping it for people who are likely to kill him for giving it away. Maybe he's financially desperate but he made an error. So, somewhere there's more explosives to find, another seller. It was sugar and sweetener, except the sweetener did not work.'

'Well, it's another line of attack,' said Stewart.

Macleod's mobile rang. 'Macleod!' His team watched his face start to frown and crease, and then start to become angry. 'You are with me, Hope. There's been an attack in Corran.'

Susan Fairchild looked over her shoulder at the kids in the rear of her car. Little Kerry was smiling back and starting to blow bubbles from her mouth while her son was asleep in his baby seat. It seemed like yesterday she had given birth to him and yet he was now six months old.

Returning her gaze to the road before her, she watched the small ferry pull into its loading position at the Corran slipway. Around her, the wind was causing the trees to rustle but the day was warm and she felt keen to take her daughter up onto the upper sides of the ferry so she could look out at the loch before them.

Her husband had promised to meet her at Glenuig for a two-night stay before he had to travel on his boat again. John was a decent man, but she hated how often he was off on his fishing boat. In truth they were struggling for money, but Susan felt it essential that the children saw their father as often as they could. John's dream of being a man of the sea and not the office accountant he had originally chosen to be, was proving to be one that was costly to more than himself.

Ahead of her, Susan watched as the line of cars began to drive onto the ferry and she followed an NHS car on before parking up. Grabbing her kids from the rear of the car, she led them up the steps at the side of the ferry onto the small split deck where she plonked herself in an orange plastic seat. Beside her, Kerry, three years of age and a quiet child, sat on one of the seats, looking so small as her legs struggled to clear the base.

The wind pushed Susan's blonde hair across her face and as she swept it away, she saw the last of the cars being parked and a queue remaining on the top of the slipway. Although it was now past lunchtime, the area was busy with tourists and Susan was thankful to have got through the large queue and to be on her way. She heard the engines fire up more strongly and anticipated the ferry moving away. At either end, the ramps which provided access on and off the ferry, were now both raised.

The raised seated area was busy, and Susan watched the driver of the NHS car stand beside her and give a smile when he saw Kerry blowing bubbles from her mouth. Susan held Archie, her baby son, in her arms and declined to show him the view of the loch as he was sleeping peacefully. Her shoulders slumped as she finally realised she would get five minutes peace.

Something whooshed beside her, and she saw the NHS man reel, bounce off the fixture behind him, and then slump forward where he tipped over the guard rail and tumbled to the deck below. Before Susan could scream, more whooshing sounds could be heard, and she instinctively wrapped Archie in her arms before spinning off her seat to cover her daughter. Kerry was screaming and Susan did not know what to do. The ferry's engines were now roaring and passengers were screaming on the deck.

Looking across to her right, she saw a woman impaled by the leg to the white wall of the deck. Blood was coming from the wound and the woman was yelling as she stood there. Beside her, feathered bolts were sticking out of the white and Susan heard more peppering the ferry. As much as she wanted to remain as small as possible, her curiosity made her turn her head and she saw a figure in the trees past the car park. From this distance it was indistinct but there seemed to be many people on the shore fleeing from this person. More whooshing sounds came, along with little dinks of metal being struck but then came several splashes.

Susan turned now and saw the car deck with many people

lying prone and a crewman trying to attend to the NHS man who had fallen off the higher deck. But there was no movement from the man and Susan then looked into the eyes of the woman screaming beside her, the bolt still sticking out from her leg. The tall lady, in a pair of jeans and a beige jumper was in her later years of life but the terror in her eyes lit up her face until she passed out, possibly from pain and she tumbled to the deck awkwardly, the flesh ripping in her leg as she fell.

Susan had Archie held tight and Kerry was before her wide-eyed and full of tears. She could not help anyone with her kids needing her. But then she pulled out her mobile. Someone must have called, surely. Someone would have. Susan pressed nine three times and waited. As the operator patched her through to the police, her eyes struggled to leave the bolt in the deck wall just four inches to the side of Kerry. As the call taker on the other end of the line asked her what was wrong, Susan found herself becoming choked up, her throat going dry and she trembled at the sight of the bolt.

'Corran ferry. People dead.' It was all she could manage.

Chapter 11

Macleod stood at the top of the slipway, large portable lights illuminating the grey concrete which led down to the unfortunate ferry below. Although it was the height of summer, the twilight hours of a lackadaisical darkness still required some form of additional brightness. Across from him, he saw Parry. The man was a flurry of activity, going from officer to officer, pointing at this and that. Macleod had been asked to sift through the witnesses and then report back to Parry on any findings about the shooter of the crossbow. The man had told Macleod that he believed there was an Irish group behind it all, aiming to cause panic and mayhem, some terrorist organisation directly in opposition to Scotland as a nation.

Macleod was not so sure, so having organised his team to interview the survivors, he had come to the scene of the attack to try to garner a better idea of what was really happening. When Parry had asked about his presence, he had simply pointed out that he needed first-hand experience to better understand the statements. This was nonsense as he had been across this ferry several times in his life.

Jona Nakamura was on scene and Macleod thought the woman looked strained. Between her teams coming to her with questions and the interruptions of Parry and his people, she hardly got a moment's peace to get on with her job. A large step up from her previous days under Mackintosh's shadow. Macleod had suggested to Parry about additional help for the forensic teams, but he had been blown off and was finding Parry difficult to deal with. So, he had gone to his senior officer and friend, DCI Dalwhinnie and she said she would take his idea under consideration.

The shooter had been positioned across from the ferry and beyond the carpark on the edge of the water. Bystanders had fled but a few had seen the person and Macleod now walked to that car park and looked at the shot the attacker would have had. He was no expert in crossbows, but he found it strange how many survivors there were on the ferry considering the shooter had the element of surprise and a stable position to fire from. Maybe Parry was right about a radical group as they did not always have the expertise in weaponry that a professional hit man would have.

There had been two persons killed and another person injured. Kyle Forsythe had been a foot passenger on holiday and walking in the area on his own. His driving licence had provided his information and it seemed he was something of a loner, a librarian from Kirkcaldy. The other deceased man was Peter Chen, a nurse in the NHS travelling with work on a weekly journey he made. The ferry man was able to identify him straight away to officers and had actually been in a shocked state over the man's death.

Watching the forensic teams working beyond the car park in the area the killer would have stood, Macleod searched for Jona, but she was nowhere to be seen. Neither did he recognise the people working for forensics but then they had probably been pulled up from Glasgow and maybe even further afield. Then he heard a familiar voice behind him.

'No, it's a forensic site, not a place to have your pub lunch. Take a bit more care when you sweep there. If we miss things, then our detectives don't get a chance. Understand? Now focus!'

Macleod had not expected Mackintosh to be here so quickly but on turning around, he saw the bustling shoulders of the powder keg of a woman. But for all the shouting, there was a little less swagger to the rebuke she was giving her colleagues. And then she saw Macleod and a smile came across her lips. As she walked over, Macleod watched her flash her eyes around at the people nearby. *She's looking to see if they are staring, to see if they notice any difference.* The operation to remove Mackintosh's breast cancer had altered her shape significantly but she had chosen to wear underwear with padding that brought her back to her full figure. Macleod understood that she would feel strange, maybe not whole and he was in no way judging her for wanting to look as she did before. But he thought the real loss would be if she did not recover her inner strength.

'Inspector, where's Jona?' asked Mackintosh.

'Trying to spot her myself, Hazel.' The choice of name was deliberate. Since she had been living with Macleod and Jane, he had grown to know her better and given the pain she had shared with him, he saw her as a friend now, not a colleague. 'How are you doing, being here?'

'Don't ask; it's like everyone sees me. But the girl needs my help. I would need help running this amount of forensic work. Not easy to keep on top of it all, make sure everything's covered, and in a case of this importance. You did right by her,

Seoras.'

Before he could comment, Mackintosh pointed to the top of the slipway where Jona Nakamura was briefing Parry on some issue. Mackintosh started striding forward but Macleod grabbed her by the arm.

'That's Parry. He's running the show. Out of London with terrorist branch, so just give her a minute. You don't want to undercut her.'

'How's she been?'

'Remarkable girl, Hazel. I think she's coped excellently but this is all escalating and she needs someone to watch her back, just to keep everything covered because I think this is going to get even busier. You have experience working across the field with lots of different branches all screaming at you for something. You need to make sure she's got your ability to manage her bosses.'

'Like I manage you,' said Mackintosh with a smile. 'And don't call her a girl—her father's bad enough with that.'

'I wouldn't say it to her face, but they are all kids to us, Hazel. Another while and you and I will be watching them from the sidelines.'

'Speak for yourself, Seoras; I haven't got anything else.'

Macleod shouted at himself internally. Jane had told him to watch what he said around Hazel for he was prone to reminding her of some loss or hurt by accident. He thought his face must have given some of this anger at himself away for Mackintosh reached out for his hand and touched it briefly.

'Not your fault, Seoras—just the truth.'

A younger voice broke the awkwardness and they both turned to see the slender Jona Nakamura coming down the slipway in her white coverall. There was no holding back as

Jona threw her arms around Mackintosh who almost buckled under the force of the hug she was receiving.

'You look good, boss,' said Jona and then stepped back to reinforce the idea by giving an approving nod as she stared at Mackintosh. Then, almost as a sudden thought, she turned to Macleod. 'Inspector, do you need me?'

'Yes, but don't let me interrupt. I'm looking on your thoughts about the shooter but take five with Hazel.' Macleod turned away and strode down the slipway to the ferry. He heard the two women excitedly conversing and after a moment of excitement, they were tearing through the workings of the forensic teams. It was ten minutes later when Macleod heard a 'hello' behind him.

'Sorry, Inspector, took a bit longer than anticipated. And thank you. Hazel said you brought her out here.'

'She brought herself, Jona. Here for you, not because I asked. Still your show though. Which brings me to my question. Do you think the shooter was randomly shooting, or was there a specific target?'

'That's a tough one, Inspector. Mr Parry was asking about the pattern. He has a theory that the shooter is after foreigners but that seems a bit of a stretch. He thinks it may be someone looking to throw foreigners out of the country.'

Macleod stared at the bolts in the ferry walls, right across the upper deck. 'What did you tell him about that theory?'

'Well, the pattern of bolts—and I'm thinking our shooter was not an ace marksman—indicate one area of intense shooting and then a random dispersal.'

'How so?'

'Look at the upper deck. You have people in most of the seats as the ferry was busy. They had let people up out of the cars as it was such a good night. I believe this has been normal for a while. You could have shot at the cars, but the upper deck was the target with only the occasional shot actually low enough for the deck. If you look at the orange seat three across from the centre, that's where Peter Chen, our NHS victim was standing. That's where the concentration of bolts is. Beyond that, there's a wide spread of bolts.'

'So, he was targeted and once he was down, the shooter just went on a random shooting exercise.'

'I cannot state the order of shooting; you'll need that from the witnesses, but Keith Forsythe, the second victim was on the stairs coming down. There's hardly another bolt near him. Seems he was rather unlucky.'

'And he's white. I can see Parry's race idea but it's a bit much to say the Germans who died in the other attacks were targeted. How did they know they would be here? Peter Chen was on a weekly run. That's quite different to tourists.'

'Sir,' said Jona, 'to be honest, I think Mr Parry is clutching at whatever straw he can find. The pressure from above, namely Whitehall, is intense. I was at a briefing, only on the sidelines, but they want answers where there aren't any yet.'

'Thanks, Jona. I won't keep you any longer. And don't fall in line behind Hazel. This is your operation, not hers. She's here to help.'

Jona laughed. 'You think she'd let me hide behind her?' With that, she disappeared to her teams of white-covered officers.

It was dawn when Macleod assembled his team at the slipway, the initial interviews of all the witnesses having been completed. His idea was that it would be easier to run through what had happened on scene and he stood in the crisp air of the morning. Although the height of summer, five in the morning was still somewhat cool to Macleod. Not that you would know if you looked at his team. Hope stood in a white t-shirt and black jeans apparently not feeling the cold. Stewart's fleece lay open and Ross was in a short-sleeved shirt and tie. It was just another observation that left him feeling his age.

'The majority of witnesses say the shooter was in the trees over there,' said Hope, pointing beyond the car park. 'That's a heck of a shot. How far can crossbows fire?'

'To be accurate, you don't want to be more than about fifty yards, maybe sixty, 'said Ross. 'They can fire much further but even a professional will want it less than a hundred yards. Given what you said earlier, boss, about the ability of our shooter, I'd say he would need to be in the trees by the shore of the car park, so that ties in with the witness statements.'

'But he's no professional,' commented Stewart. 'Reckon I could do better.'

Macleod raised his eyebrows and turned to the car park. 'So, what did our witnesses from the car park say about our shooter? What descriptions did we get?'

'Bit varied,' said Hope. 'Most only saw the shooter as they turned and then the witnesses legged it up to the road. But they were in the same hoodie as our shooter at the canal. But the hood was not up. This time people say there was a snood over the head and across the nose and mouth. Also, a shock of red hair coming out the back of the snood and running down to the shoulders. Curly too.'

'Was it a male or female?' asked Macleod.

'Female,' said Stewart. 'I had several say it was a female; after all, you had the long red hair.'

'What about the figure of the shooter?' asked Macleod.

'As I said, female, sir'

'No, Stewart, did anyone mention hips, legs, bottom, maybe even boobs—anything that confirmed the shooter as a woman?'

'Build was similar to our canal shooter in that there was no real male or female definition—androgynous, really.' Hope stared at Macleod as she said it. 'But the bomber was definitely female, wasn't she, sir? I mean she had female definition in abundance.'

'As far as the CCTV shows, McGrath.'

'Hang on,' said Hope. 'Are you saying that these are not different people? It's a bit of a stretch.'

'I'm not saying, McGrath; I'm keeping an open mind. Mr Parry is talking about a terrorist group, but no publicity has been forthcoming. These groups feed off fear and usually want some sort of social change or revenge. And they want the world to see their cause. There's only a claim of an unheard-of, dissident, Irish paramilitary group.'

'But we have different suspects, sir,' said Ross. 'The bomber is not the same person as our canal shooter.'

'At the moment, it looks like that.' Macleod was aware of his team's scepticism but did not appreciate Hope's raised eyebrows. 'But we are struggling on motive. We know nothing about our killers except one uses a gun, poorly, one plants a half-arsed bomb, and now we have an amateur crossbow shooter. Why change up? Why not stick with and get better with the gun?'

'I get there's confusion on the motive, sir, but I think the same person idea is a bit stretched.'

'At the moment, McGrath, I'll give you that but let's look at our victims. What connection is there between them?'

Stewart stepped forward this time. 'We have tourists and an

NHS worker. All a bit random, is it not?'

'Yes, it looks that way but get into them Stewart, into everything, ferret me out something.'

'Sir.'

McGrath turned to her DCs. 'Stewart, Ross, get me a distance on those shots and then run through the statements to see if we can track where the killer went from the undergrowth by the car park. Maybe we can help forensics narrow down some of the sites they should be combing more closely.' There were nods and Hope watched the junior members of the team leave before turning to her boss.

'Seoras, where are you going with this? It sounds like a wild goose chase you're on. Surely Parry is right, there's a group co-ordinating this. What is telling you different?'

'Gut, Hope, just gut instinct. And also, since when did we get terrorists attacking such out-of-the way places? These are not soft targets; they are almost random. Shoot people one minute and then blow up a bridge. All done with a sense of the amateur.'

'Parry was looking at Irish terrorists, possibly.'

'Again Hope, where's the neon sign saying, here we are, and this is what you're doing wrong? I get it looks like some mad terrorist, but generally mad ones don't exist. They have reasons, however strange to us; they have beliefs and reasons.'

'Okay, we'll keep this as an open line of enquiry,' said Hope, 'but don't publicise it higher up or we'll look crazy.'

Macleod rolled his eyes at her. 'Gut is telling me I'm right, Hope. Experience tells me never to present ideas to senior officers that come purely from your gut. I'm not stupid.'

'You have been under pressure lately with the whole Mack-intosh thing and that. I'm just covering the bases like you say you need me to.'

Macleod turned away and walked down the slipway, giving Hope a frosty shoulder. But then he shouted over his shoulder, 'Yes, I did say that. I'll give you that.'

Chapter 12

The room was a sterile affair with coffee in canteens on a table at one end and a number of desks in a square, each with a chair behind it. Every chair was the same, the metallic frame contrasting with the deep red fabric, all topped off with a black trim. It matched the décor on the wall, right down to the red stripe that traversed the walls at shoulder height. Everything about it said commercial hotel for the traveling businessman.

With the travel between the three scenes of crime, it was becoming difficult to have a central operations room and Macleod had made the decision to pull his senior team into a Fort William hotel for the evening, away from all distractions. On the table were all the witness statements from each attack, and Hope was watching her two junior colleagues gaze at them. Like most hotel conference rooms, especially the smaller ones, it was hot and almost claustrophobic.

Earlier, Macleod and Hope had been part of a conference call on the internet between all the senior officers involved in the cases. Parry from the terrorist division had been showing the current line of thought, that a band of rogue nationalists were at fault for these outrages. Every time he spoke, Macleod reckoned Parry had a new theory. Macleod had put forward his theory that it could actually be one person and that because the identification by CCTV and by those who witnessed the killings first hand was so poor, they could not run with this particular theory just yet.

His interjection had not gone down well, especially with Parry, and Hope felt that Macleod's direct line report, DCI Marjorie Dalwhinnie had somewhat sidelined him in the ensuing conversation for his own good. He had then been called on the landline by the DCI twenty minutes after the conference call had finished. Hope was not used to seeing an agitated Macleod, and apart from their difficult case on Barra, he had always seemed in control. But this whole approach to solving this case was bothering him immensely and Hope heard him raise his voice to the DCI, something Seoras was not in the habit of doing.

During the call, Macleod's team had been directed to try to identify the perpetrators from the descriptions given by the witnesses, a slap in the face by Parry, who advised his own branch would put out proper feelers and shake down some undercover assets in various quarters. Hope believed the instruction to Macleod was meant to annoy him, but it was what the boss had wanted to do anyway, and they had already hired the hotel room. A sketch artist was en route to the hotel to try and piece together some of their findings, although Hope was unsure that the artist would have much material to go on.

'Do they deliberately crack the heating on? It's summer,' complained Ross. Hope watched him remove his jacket and lose his tie over the back of the chair, before rolling up his sleeves and then opening the top two buttons on his shirt. Dependable Ross was his name at the station, which Hope thought of as unfair for the man was more than a dependable officer. His broad chest and wide shoulders along with a taut face gave him the look of a pirate, if only he would get into less sombre clothes. If Ross had been inclined to women, Hope thought, she might even have tried to get to know him on a more personal level.

Across the desk from him, Stewart was peering at a report like it was about to self-destruct in the next ten seconds. She swept along lines of text so quickly that Hope wondered if there was some part of her brain that had been replaced with a computer, allowing her to take in vast quantities of information at pace. Macleod had been right about her—she was a ferret, and a good one.

The door of the room swung open and hit the table behind it. Hope looked up to see Macleod with a face of thunder.

'Get me something. Stewart. Ross, get me some sort of damn picture of these people and prove I'm on a real path with my theory before I get placed in the dunce corner.'

'Sir?' asked Hope raising an eyebrow.

'They don't believe me, Hope, even Dalwhinnie. And she knows I have a point. We know so little they can't just go off on the theory of a terrorist group.'

'They can't dismiss it either.'

'No, but they need to give this idea more credence. The lone wolf line needs to be a major line of enquiry. Instead, we're getting pulled on to it, just the four of us, and Parry's pulling everyone else on the search for a new terrorist group. You heard him on the call.'

Hope flashed her eyes at their junior colleagues sitting at the arranged tables and Macleod took the hint.

'Stewart, Ross, like I said, find me something.' With that,

Macleod took Hope to one side. 'I've been detached, put off to the side for clarity of investigation. They don't want the main investigation compromised so we are going to run this line of enquiry separately. Everything uploaded onto the central investigation database but run as a separate line. They might as well take me off the case.'

'So why didn't they?' asked Hope.

'Because Dalwhinnie is scared I might be right. Parry gave her an earful because I didn't toe the line during that call. We would be back in Inverness but Marjorie Dalwhinnie has known me too long. She's giving me a chance to prove my theory.'

'But if it's not right, you'll look like ...'

'Yes, the idiot who went off on one. Apparently, Parry told her my retirement was overdue.'

'That's a bit crappy,' said Hope. 'Guess he's not used to someone standing up too hard against him.'

'I don't know how long we'll get this rope with which to hang myself so let's get on with it. How are you going about the ID collection?'

Hope showed Macleod the three piles of witness statements and the sheets of paper representing the three attacks. On the recording sheets were sections for definite descriptions and then a separate section for those seen around the area, people unknown to the witnesses.

The four detectives worked on the statements for the next four hours, during which time Macleod was informed that his sketch artist had been re-directed to a different case and would be with him as soon as he could. At ten o'clock, Macleod ordered food for everyone and they continued until Stewart stated she needed air. Given it was now just shy of midnight,

Macleod told them all to take ten minutes and then they would come back and round up what they had before getting some sleep.

As Hope was about to leave the room which now only contained Macleod and herself, she was almost knocked back as the door opened to reveal Mackintosh. At first her face smiled and then she saw Hope and it became demure.

'Evening, Sergeant,' said the forensic officer.

'Is Jona with you?' asked Hope.

'Stuck with Parry and his teams. I'm catching some rest in case she needs help early tomorrow.'

Hope nodded, a little disappointed at not seeing her friend but then she felt Macleod touch her shoulder.

'Give us a moment, please, McGrath.'

Hope nodded and walked out of the door which was promptly shut behind her. She knew the polite thing to do was simply to walk outside and get some air. But some curiosity made her halt and she heard tears from the room she had just left. Macleod was not saying anything, but Hope was sure he probably had Mackintosh on his shoulder. The tears were now very audible. 'They can tell when they look at me,' were the only words, Hope caught.

When she returned to the room ten minutes later, one could not have told there had been any breakdown from Mackintosh or that Macleod had been performing his support act. Instead, the forensic officer was sitting behind one of the desks on the opposite side of the formed square from Macleod who had a number of sheets in front of him.

'Okay, Stewart, break down our findings from tonight for us.' All eyes swung to the diminutive but feisty woman who pushed her glasses up her nose and stepped in front of a whiteboard, pen in hand.

'Right, the canal shooter we have truly little on. All witnesses fail to say whether it was a man or woman with any degree of positivity. Some say a man, but they have not backed that up with a facial sighting. Indeed, most describe the build as sinewy, or thin. No defining features of male or female traits. The hooded top was well enough fixed that the face was not seen at all and the cameras got nothing. The killer walked with head down until reaching the designated point and then a gun was raised in front of it.'

'Okay, so at this point it could be anyone who doesn't have great definition,' said Hope.

'And who is about five foot six,' said Stewart.

'Go on, Stewart, what about the bombing?' asked Macleod.

'Well, the CCTV shows a suspect who was female. Long hair and a generous bosom, shaved legs. All the witnesses who saw the bomber state she was female although most got only a quick look and very few actually saw her without some sort of object in the way, like the car when she was pretending to change the wheel.'

'So, it's definitely someone different,' said Hope, 'after all, the figure is different. You don't hide a bosom like that under a hoodie.'

'That's a fair point, Hope,' said Macleod, 'if it's real.'

'Is there anything to say it's not?'

'Actually,' said Ross, 'there is.' Reaching forward into a pile of statements, Ross dove through them, until he grasped one in his hands and then flipped it open. After scanning through the text, he kept his finger on a line as he looked up with delight on his face. 'There's a section here, from an Andrew Houghton. Comments about the bomber's figure. 'Great cleavage but it must have been locked in tight because it didn't move properly.' Seems he agreed with you, boss.'

'What sort of a guy notices that?' blurted out Mackintosh.

'Come on, he's a guy,' retorted Stewart before realising she had said it out loud.

'Okay,' said Macleod, 'Stewart and Ross, you can go see Mr Houghton and see if he's simply a pervert or actually is a most observant witness. What about our third killer?'

'Hold on, sir. One other thing about number two. From the camera, the suspect was around five feet six.'

The room went quiet. Macleod's fist gripped and his arm shook gently as if he knew he was onto something. 'Good, now number three, Stewart.'

'Well, this is more difficult as very few actually were able to give anything useful as the witnesses were generally fleeing the scene, but we know the perpetrator had a hoodie on like in the first attack.'

'What about the height?' asked Hope.

'The reports were very sketchy and those that offered a height range said from five feet four to 'under six feet'. So, it's not a definite match but is still a possibility. Again, no facial sighting, only the covered figure.'

'So, the conclusion is that while a single person carrying out all three attacks is not confirmed, there is a possibility, if they can pretend to be a woman,' said Hope.

'They could be a woman,' said Ross, 'but altered their chest to look different. You can get prosthetics for that area.'

Hope could not help but glance at Mackintosh and saw the woman staring stonily ahead. Macleod never even looked, and Ross seemed oblivious to any awkwardness, as did Stewart.

'What else did we find out about people in the vicinity before and after?' asked Macleod, again never turning to Mackintosh. 'Do we have any other coincidences? Any other sightings of someone out of place?'

'Not so much out of place but someone at both scenes. A man wearing combat trousers and camouflage t-shirt at the roadside near Corran, and along the canal, higher up than Neptune's Staircase.'

'Why is he of interest, Stewart?' asked Hope.

'Well, he normally wouldn't be except I'm looking for a distinct figure. The person was seen by only one witness at either scene and both times before the attack. He was not doing anything suspicious and it's the camouflage outfit that made the witnesses recall him. In both instances, there was a bag over the person's shoulder, a large duffel. Camouflage bag, too. He didn't do anything out of the ordinary, but his physical description makes him interesting.'

'How?' asked Ross.

'Both witnesses state they are around five feet six; both state the man as sinewy.'

'Hope, tomorrow, those witnesses. I want them back in for questioning with the sketch artist.'

'Sir,' said Hope, 'I will do but there's no proof it's a single person operation. We still have the bomb blast. We're postulating about that one—there's no proof.'

'We've truly little proof of anything. I'm postulating as much as Parry, Hope. But we need to follow it. Let's get on it tomorrow. Get some rest everyone, and good work.'

Hope watched her colleagues tidy up and pack away the statements into boxes. When they had completed, she followed Ross to his room where they stored the boxes. He refused the offer of a drink so Hope made her way down to the small reception area and asked for a hot chocolate before spying Macleod outside. As her chocolate arrived, Hope saw Stewart, dressed in a crop top and shorts, heading for the hotel gym.

'Little late?' queried Hope.

'Need to wind down after that. No better way than to punch it out.'

Hope laughed as the woman left and then grabbed her hot chocolate and decided to take it outside to speak with her boss. She was not on the same line of thought as him with his single-person theory, but she wanted him to know she would back him, even if she was not convinced.

As she exited the front door, Hope saw Macleod standing beside a pillar but as she drew closer, she realised someone else was there. As she turned on her heel, Hope heard sobbing and the husky voice of Mackintosh.

'He said prosthetics, Seoras. Could he tell?'

'No, Hazel, just a coincidence. You look great. Trust me, you are still the same woman.'

'Bullshit, Seoras. You're a bad liar.'

Chapter 13

The following morning started brightly, the sun rising early and filling Fort William with the joy of summer. Hope had decided to get out early for a run and the only downer on the morning was that Jona was too tired to accompany her. Her friend and colleague was under severe stress from her workload and their moments to speak had been few and far between. In typical fashion, Jona Nakamura was hiding the tension well and had a serene look to her but the eyes were showing a fatigue that Jona never had in normal times.

Hope accelerated her pace for the last mile of her run, driving her legs hard and letting the oxygen pump through her lungs. It was good to feel this free, this alive, especially when she was up against a mental block in this case. It was also strange working underneath the umbrella of other units, namely the terrorist branch. Normally Macleod would have an almost-free rein in solving a case, his experience counting for so much to his superiors. His success rate was also a key factor but the teams from the south did not know him that way and the entire Inverness team felt like small cogs in an enormous wheel.

As Hope reached the hotel and started to slow down, she saw Ross emerging from the front door to shake hands with a greying man in his forties. As ever, Ross was smooth and professional as he accompanied the man inside the building and Hope took a moment to sit on a wooden bench in the grounds of the hotel. Sweat dripped off her and the Lycra she wore clung tight to her skin. Her idea that a moment on the bench would help her cool down did not seem to be working and she decided that a cold shower would be best and made to stand until her mobile rang.

'McGrath here.'

Hello, ma'am, it's Sergeant Anderson. I've just come on shift and there's been an accident in Munlochy, near one of the shops.'

'Okay,' said Hope, 'how can I help?'

'Well, a woman has been hit by a bus and she's in a bad way, on her way to Raigmore hospital. It's just that one of the boys at the scene clocked the address from her purse and thought it was similar to your DI's home. I didn't want to disturb him with all that's going on especially if we are up a blind alley. He's so secretive about his personal life so I thought you might know.'

Hope's throat tightened. 'What's the address?' The Sergeant passed over the details. 'How bad?' asked Hope, realising that the address was indeed Macleod's home.

'She's in a critical condition, Ma'am. I'll ring him directly.'

'No, Sergeant, I'm at his hotel. I'll tell him myself.' Hope hung up and ran inside the hotel. Racing through the foyer in her Lycra, she saw Ross who gave her a strange stare. 'Follow me,' she shouted and then tore up the stairs to the floor Macleod's room was on. Arriving at the bland wooden door, she banged hard on it.

'What's the crisis?' asked Macleod, opening the door quickly.

'Jane, sir,' blurted Hope, struggling to catch her breath, 'she's been knocked down, on her way to Raigmore. You need to go. She's not good.'

Ross arrived behind Hope, breathing heavily and on hearing what she was saying announced, 'I'll get a marked car to drive you,' and then ran back down the corridor.

Macleod reeled in the doorway. 'Jane? How is she?'

'Not good, sir, I don't know the exact details but we'll get you there quickly. You need to go!'

'But I can't leave you? Not with this mess to sort. I can't …'

'Yes, you bloody can,' shouted Hope. 'Grab your jacket and whatever else you need; we'll sort the rest.'

'But the case, the killer, we don't have a real idea …'

'Trust me, Seoras. Trust Ross and trust Stewart. Trust us. Go to Jane; she needs you.'

The man was clearly struggling to focus, and Hope grabbed his arm taking him inside and gently forced him to sit on the bed. Grabbing his coat and a few other items, she knelt before him and looked into his eyes. His face was white.

'I can't lose her. I can't go there again,' he blurted.

'She's not dead, Seoras,' said Hope and pulled his head to her chest holding him tight. 'You need to be with her.'

In a moment he had gone from her tough and tacit boss to a mere child struggling to comprehend the world as it spun. Her heart ached for him, but Jane was not dead, and there was so much they did not know. Hope wanted to simply get a car and drive him there. When she had first met him, she had held him in a hotel corridor as he crumbled at the memory of his deceased wife's suicide. Now she saw the same hurt and panic return.

'Car's outside,' said Ross, sticking his head around the door.

'Stand up, Seoras, come on, you need to go,' said Hope and helped her boss to his feet. Ross picked up the man's coat and Hope, still in her running gear, walked him through the hotel to the awaiting car at the front of the hotel. His feet were laden, and she had to hold him a few times as he stumbled. It was striking how a man who stood up to death and truly awful situations in his day job, simply crumbled when it was his nearest and dearest involved. As Hope tried to usher Macleod into the passenger seat of the car, he stopped and turned to her, taking her shoulders in his hands and then leaning in towards her ear.

'The man in the camouflage, chase him. They want a group, some sort of organisation but trust me, Hope—chase the loner on this one. I feel it, this is personal, this is a man with a reason, a good one. At least to him.'

'I hear you, sir, but don't worry; you need to go.'

Macleod shook his head. 'Listen. You need to step up and look at the whole now, you need to do what I do. Lean on Ross and be tight as a pair. They will try to take you off the scent. They're not seeing it; when I told them, they didn't want to believe it. Hunt and get the evidence. Be a rock, Hope, or you won't get him.'

Macleod lifted his head back and stared at her before turning to Ross. 'Back her like she backs me, Ross.' With that, he stepped into the passenger seat and closed the door. The car sped off leaving Hope standing in her running gear, her body still sweating though now it was from shock and tension.

'I need to contact Dalwhinnie,' said Hope. 'Parry, too. Organise what's happening, get onto these witnesses and see the sketch artist. Have a word with Stewart and then Jona and Mackintosh.'

'Stop!' said Ross. 'You need to do one thing, boss. Get upstairs and get in your shower and just take stock and get cleaned up. Then I'll meet you down here. I'll take care of telling everyone, I will sort it. You can talk to them when you are good and ready, and not in a state of shock about what's just happened.'

'No, I can't. There's too much to do.'

'It's what you would tell Macleod to do if he was like this. You're not alone just because you have the hot seat.'

Hope looked at Ross who was smiling at her and regarding her with admiration. She was used to men giving her an admiring glance, but they often saw only the physical exterior. But Ross was not interested in her looks or shape. Maybe he was one of only a few men she knew who would not be influenced by her feminine demeanour. Macleod was right; maybe she needed to lean on him from the off.

'Shower, Ross. I'll be down in half an hour. Spread the word to whoever we need. And tell them I'm happy to step up.'

'Yes, boss,' said Ross, smiling. 'By the way, do you think he's right, about the loner with an agenda?'

'I don't know but you know Macleod. Never easy to work with but he can read people and situations. I can't see it myself but, … who knows?'

'I wouldn't back against him, boss. Doubt they'll see it that way. We need some evidence.'

'Then go get some, Ross. Macleod once told me Stewart was a little ferret. Let's use her in what she's good at. Then you and I will have to piece it together.'

Ross nodded and walked back into the hotel. A chill ran down Hope's spine and she knew it did not come from a lack of heat. She'd always had top cover, always worked with a net,

113

someone above her. And yes, there were still people over her now, but they were at odds with her boss's theory. She'd need to become an operator, like Macleod, someone who worked the line that was needed while keeping the upper management happy.

As she walked back into the hotel, Hope felt her own feet become laden and the chill was not leaving her. Three attacks had happened and more could follow. Macleod had clearly stated he thought that Parry and his team would not catch whoever was responsible. It was falling on her. She would not let him down. She could not. As she stood in her cold shower, Hope let her mind unwind and everything that was bottled up raced across her inner vision. When she emerged from the shower, Hope prayed she would have a clearer view on what was happening.

* * *

Hope pressed the button that cancelled the conference call she was on. For the last half hour, she had been listening to Parry pulling together the evidence from the various attack sites and struggled to dispassionately disagree with him. Macleod had no evidence to say this was the same person other than all attackers being of roughly the same height and two of them having the same hoodie. Maybe the hoodie was to be a trademark and the bomber had not worn one because it would have stuck out. There had been a group previously unheard of claiming they had carried out the attacks, but Parry said his undercover personnel were thick into finding out exactly where the attacks had come from.

Hope had mentioned the possibility of a lone attacker, but

Parry was dismissive while DCI Dalwhinnie pointed to the number of methods being used and asked why the person would not simply use the same tried-and-trusted technique. With no answer forthcoming, Hope had decided to simply keep her head below the parapet and work further on her theories. One thing was for sure—they were now to be more like foot soldiers rather than detectives in this case.

Ross knocked on the door and entered, smiling as ever in his simple way. It was not the smile of an exuberant clown or of an overzealous pastor, rather that of a simple friend.

'Bit rough was it, boss?' he asked.

'The DI has his theories and he keeps on line with them because he's usually so certain. I'm not Ross, not at all. It's hard to sit and defend what you're doing when you're not sure it's right.'

'Then don't be him, sir, be yourself. If you don't know, then say it. If it's sensitive, keep it to yourself. There's nothing to stop you following a line quietly until you know it to be true. Especially with so many parties involved.'

Hope nodded. Macleod had called Ross *dependable* and that description was extremely accurate. The man covered the bases well, and while he did not have the investigative nose of Stewart, he did see the big picture quickly when ideas were floated.

'Did you know that Macleod calls me Hope when we are alone, Ross? He almost drops the ranks.'

Ross put his hand to his mouth and coughed. 'We all know you are close, not in any incorrect way, just that you have been through so much, in fact it's like you're his ... ' Ross stopped. 'Sorry, my mind wandered. Like I said, we know you are close.'

'His what?' asked Hope, almost laughing.

'It wouldn't be right to say.'

'You put it there, Ross. Tell me. That's an order if it helps.'

'Well, like his boy. You know, an apprentice. Squire even.'

Hope could see Ross squirming. The man must have been busy to let the idea even float from his mouth.

'Why are you still a Detective Constable, Ross? You've been here longer than me. You should be a Sergeant.'

'I'm happy enough.'

'Does anyone call you Alan? I mean anyone on the force.' Ross shook his head. 'Well, I need a second I can trust and share with, so it's Alan now, if that's okay with you and in here, alone, it will be Hope.'

'Yes, sir.'

'How are the reports coming? I take it you've sent everything up the line.' Ross nodded. 'Good.'

'Heard anything about the boss's woman?'

'No,' said Hope. 'I haven't even had a chance to ring.'

'Well I did a few hours ago. He said she was into theatre. Touch and go. I just wondered if there had been any more.'

Hope kicked herself for not finding the time. As ever, Ross had everything in his hands, all complete and dealt with while she was feeling a bit asunder. 'What happened exactly?'

'Crossing the road and hit by a bus that could not stop for some reason. Took her off her feet and threw her up the road. Apparently, they were surprised she survived this far.'

'Dear God, I'll have to ring him. Before you go, get Stewart to set up a database and start filling in details of everyone at the scenes. I mean every detail you can get. Any link no matter how obscure. She's perfect for it. We have victims, albeit from different countries, and I find it hard to believe this is all random. That part of Macleod's analysis rings true to me. No banner waving high, no bugle call rallying people to a cause. He might just be right that this is personal.'

'I'll get her straight on to it. I guess there will be work done on this already by the other teams.'

'Do this in house, just us. Until we know something, I want to make it look like I'm following the line being taken above us.'

'Understood. And one more thing, boss.'

'What, Alan?'

Ross stepped forward until he was right in front of the desk Hope was sitting behind. 'You do realise that he knows you can do this?'

'Of course, I know Macleod trusts me.'

'That's not what I said. I said he knows you,' and Ross pointed his finger, 'can do this. If he didn't, he would have called Dalwhinnie by now. You would not be sitting here.'

Hope raised her eyebrows. 'He's got enough on his plate to be thinking about the case.'

'Two hours, or so, in a car, you bet he would have called. Have you even had a call from the DCI?' Hope shook her head. 'Then he's called her to say leave you in charge.'

Ross gave his smile, the simple friendly one and turned away. Hope felt an immense pride from the words but underneath there was also a growing fear. What if she did not live up to his belief in her?

Hope pulled out her mobile and rang Macleod's number. The phone rang four times and then the call was cut off by the other party. *Of course, he's busy. Poor Seoras.*

Chapter 14

Sarah Doonan stepped out of the small corner shop with three ice creams in her hand. As she walked across the road, one of them leaked onto her hand and dripped onto the top of her hiking boots. The sun was providing an oppressive heat and Sarah wondered just how intact the ice cream would be when she reached her small family.

This was their first holiday in forever and now with Martin's promotion to the higher echelons of middle management, she hoped they could go on more holidays like this. Her daughter, Ambrosia, now sixteen and sporting a ring through her nose, needed some stability after the incident with 'Tadger', that spitefully obnoxious young man. He had been fortunate that Martin had caught him with their daughter. If Sarah had been there, the boy would be a eunuch by now.

Not that Ambrosia had been entirely blameless, wearing things that any young man would have been hard pushed to not be turned on by. But she was too young, and the older boy should have known better. If the publicity from it had not be so potentially bad, Sarah would have seen the little turd put behind bars.

But there was nothing out here so repugnant and Ambrosia had been in a decent mood if not entirely happy. Martin was also in good spirits but then Sarah had been an attentive wife, a reward for his hard work at getting the promotion. Yes, she would bring this family together, haul them up into the limelight of success, a model for others to follow.

Martin stood at the slipway and took the ice cream from his wife, watching his daughter mope about at the end of the concrete structure. 'Don't get yourself wet,' he shouted. 'The ends can be covered in algae. You won't even see the problem before you are in the water.' His black-jacketed daughter did not look round but instead stepped even closer, so her black boots now splashed the edge of the river.

'Don't say anything else,' said Sarah. 'She's here and she's not been too bad at all. She's only used the F-word once. She is trying.'

'Well maybe she shouldn't call her father a …'

'No. Enough Martin. We are on holiday and we are going to enjoy it and get on like a proper family. So, keep it light and happy. You might enjoy yourself. And if you don't, you'll enjoy tonight anyway.'

Martin had been quite a catch for Sarah, who, although coming from a council estate, had never considered herself to be anything but worthy of a castle or a country house. On the other hand, Martin's parents owned a house worth nearly a half million pounds and despite not being on altogether convivial terms with their son, had influence in the world of hospital management.

'I'm not happy with what I did, Sarah. I mean, there were better uses for that money. I'm sure people needed it.'

'And we needed you to do what you did. And look, a year later, you are rewarded with a chance to run an entire sector of hospitals. There's no point worrying about other people,

Martin, because you would have got no thanks for not placing that money where Francine wanted it. You're on the up, and so are we. I think Ambrosia will love her new swimming pool.'

'Probably use it for an orgy when we're away.'

'Enough, Martin.' Sarah stared hard at her husband who dropped his shoulders and lost himself in his ice cream. Turning to her daughter, she called, 'Ambrosia, honey. Your ice cream is running.' Watching the shaved head turn, Sarah sighed. After this holiday, she was going to get her daughter sorted. The girl would learn how to dress properly, sophisticatedly, so she could land herself a man who would do her proud. A man she could rule over. Sarah knew how and she would teach her daughter.

There was a twang. It was like a guitar string being plucked except there was no note from it. It was also in the distance and if the air were not so still Sarah believed she would not have heard it. But then there was a clatter beside her.

Martin started looking around him as his daughter swore from the end of the pier.

'Less of that tongue,' said Sarah but then jumped in shock as she saw an arrow lying beside her. There was another twang in the air and shortly after another clatter, but this time it was to her other side.

'Someone's shooting!' cried Martin, grabbing his wife by the arm.

'From where?' yelled Sarah.

There was another twang and it seemed like it was above them. Sarah turned to look at the bridge that crossed Loch Leven at Balachulish. It was a road bridge but at the moment, she could see a car parked on it and someone standing beside it, holding a bow.

'Arggh!' It was Ambrosia and her daughter tumbled to the ground. Martin threw himself over the girl and as Sarah stood, frozen in panic, she saw more arrows being fired towards her. Her eyes saw the latest one sail over her head and then a cry came from the pavement behind her. A young child was being held by their father, an arrow coming out of her shoulder.

A car accelerated behind Sarah and she started to run towards the shop she had been in only a few minutes before. As she ran, she continually glanced behind her at her husband and child. She caught her foot and fell, coming down hard on the road. Someone grabbed her and a car flew past. In her daze she saw Ambrosia lying on the slipway, her father leaning over her. Then she saw an arrow falling from the sky. It happened so quickly she had no time to shout, no chance to scream. Instead, she gave a muffled cry as the arrow barely missed her husband but buried itself in the back of her child.

Someone was now running towards Ambrosia, a green first aid case in hand. On the bridge, she heard someone beeping a car horn and the archer had disappeared. The car the attacker had stood beside was now driving away across the bridge and Sarah saw another car in pursuit. Trying to run to her daughter, her legs collapsed again and she hit the road hard. There were more shouts as her eyes closed and she drifted off to blackness.

* * *

Ross was looking through database searches with Stewart when his mobile vibrated in his pocket. Pulling it out, he recognised a call from the main police operations centre and then listened intently as he was advised of another attack. The incident was taking place in Ballachulish, and Ross recognised the place well, having driven across the bridge there many times on his way to Oban. The distance to the attack site was short, being just beyond Corran where the ferry attack had taken place. As he ran to Hope's temporary office, she was already emerging, jacket being flung around her shoulders, her red ponytail swinging behind her.

'Grab the car, Ross, and bring Stewart, too. I'd like to get there before Parry's crawling all over it.'

Ross nodded, turned on his heel and shouted for Stewart before continuing out of the building for the car. Once inside the vehicle, he brought it to the front of the hotel they were staying in and waited for his colleagues. Hope pushed open the hotel front doors, her mobile to her ear and was closely followed by Stewart, dwarfed by her near-six-feet boss but displaying as much hustle as the taller woman.

The drive to the bridge at Ballachulish took them along Loch Linnhe, past the Corran Ferry, and then to the entrance to Loch Leven. Although a well-built single road, the corners made overtaking hard and on arrival at the bridge, Ross found it hard to negotiate the blockage up ahead of cars, the bridge having been closed off by the local police.

Abandoning the car on the north side of the bridge, the threesome made their way past the police cordon to find that Parry had already beaten them to it. Realising she had been spotted by him, Hope made her way directly to the senior officer.

'Sir, what's the story?'

'Unsure at the moment, Sergeant, but it looks like a copycat to me. I mean the attacker is using a bow and arrow and made a right hash of it if they were trying to kill someone. There's a teenage girl injured, although it's not too deep a wound, and a young child who has an arrow through her shoulder. Both will be all right but it's a random way to hit someone.'

'Sounds it, sir. Do you want us to take charge or have you got it covered?'

Hope watched the man staring around him, almost calculating something. As she stood awaiting an answer, he made no effort to engage her but rather took in his own thoughts and summations on the scene.

'Take charge, McGrath. I think this is a copycat so I'm going to get back onto the other incidents and our sources. Do the necessary—statements and forensics—and if there is anything that confirms it as our terrorist group then I want to know straight away. But I doubt it. This has a rather amateur feel to it.'

Hope wanted to say that Macleod reckoned all the attacks had an amateur feel to them, but she thought that was hard to say if people had died at the other incidents. 'Will do, sir,' said Hope and turned to Ross, calling him over.

'It's ours for now, Ross. Get a list of all the witnesses and make sure we get statements from them all. If the attacker had a car, see if anyone clocked the number plate and get that out to the police world at large. I'm going to speak to my forensics people. I also want to speak to the senior officer who has been dealing with this in five minutes because Parry gave me very little. I want to know exactly what happened.'

Ross nodded in his efficient way and sped off to a uniformed officer nearby. Hope would need to let him get on with his work and she watched her colleague nab Stewart as he walked. Looking around her, Hope saw Jona Nakamura emerging from a car and speaking to Parry. It was a brief conversation and

123

Hope saw Jona then speak to Mackintosh who had been in the car with her. As Hope walked over to the group, Jona departed in a car with Parry leaving Mackintosh with a couple of faces Hope did not recognise. The older woman looked around and then spied Hope, making a direct line for her.

'Sergeant McGrath, I'm taking charge of forensics at the scene and Miss Nakamura advises me you have the scene. I need to get everyone clear and then cordon off the area. From what I've been told, someone fired arrows from that bridge at several people down here, injuring two. Then the person sped off in a car. I'll see what that car has left behind on the bridge if anything and see if our arrows can give us anything. Can you get the area cleared for me as soon as feasible, please?'

'Of course,' replied Hope. 'We believe this may be a copycat incident and not one carried out by the group we're looking for, so if you can eliminate this site from the larger investigation, that would be great.'

'And if it isn't, I'll get you what I can to identify them. Once you have a picture of what happened, brief me please. Now I'll get out of your way.' Mackintosh went to turn away but then stopped. 'Did you hear anything? I've rung Seoras, sorry, I mean Macleod, but he is not answering.'

'I can't reach Seoras either, but he's likely at her side and closed himself off to the world. He's besotted with her, Hazel, as I'm sure you know.' Mackintosh nodded and walked away, a sadness in her eyes.

Hope scanned the area looking for what needed attention but then stopped herself. She was in charge here and needed to step back and see what was really going on. Looking up at the bridge, she decided that would be a good place to look down on the scene from and try to map out how things had happened. But first she needed that uniformed officer who had run the incident before the cavalry arrived.

Chapter 15

The day was drawing into long summer shadows as Hope stood on the bridge looking down after a day spent in collection of evidence and witness statements. A local hall had been used to go through the statements and Stewart had been dispatched with an officer to get a statement from the injured teenager and her family. Hope had requested that an experienced archer be brought to the scene to get some sort of perspective on the ability of an average person to launch an arrow towards this target and she was awaiting the man's arrival.

As she stood alone, Hope thought of the statements she had taken that day and those reported back to her. No one had been in the area on any routine business or as a weekly or monthly attendance. Everyone seemed to be there quite randomly. The teenager who had been shot was with her parents and they had stopped for an ice cream by the water. The girl had been messing about at the water in an attempt to avoid her parents and they had said they had only decided on the day out that morning. The child who was struck by the other arrow lived on a council estate with her mother in Fort William and they had popped out for the day with the child's grandmother. Again, it seemed quite random that she should be attacked and that only gave credence to Parry's belief that this was simply another terror attack, albeit a copycat event.

'Sergeant, I have a Mr MacTavish here from the Oban archery club. He's driven a bit of a distance.' Turning to the man, Ross asked,' Can I get you something, sir?'

'Ach, no, Detective, I'm good. Let me give you what help I can and then I'll get out of your way. I'm sure you have your hands full at the moment with all this nonsense that's going on.'

Hope looked at the man and was somewhat disappointed to see a man of an older age, broad shouldered, but whose arms seemed to lack the muscles she presumed an archer would have. Thin, grey hair ran across the man's head and a white beard made him look more like a disappointing Father Christmas than the bronzed Adonis she hoped would be attending. Still, if he knew his stuff, that was what mattered.

'Mr MacTavish, DS McGrath. Thank you for coming out so promptly; I am grateful.'

'Jim, none of that mister stuff, just Jim.'

'How long have you been an archer?' asked Hope, shaking his hand.

'Oh, since my twenties so that's, well, let's say it's at least a half century.'

'You're looking well on it.'

'And I thought you police officers were not allowed to lie. But butter me up; I can take it. So how can I help you, ma'am?'

Hope led the man to the side of the bridge and looked down at the concrete slipway below and then the road that ran along the shore. 'Imagine being up here with your bow, Jim, and you want to shoot someone down there. I need to know how experienced you would have to be, to be assured of success.'

'Is that what he did, fired arrows down there at people? Bloody hell.'

Hope could see the man was physically affected by the idea and she placed a hand on his shoulder as she watched him grasp the railings.

'Sorry, Sergeant,' said Jim, 'it's just that we don't shoot at people. We're not even allowed to target animals in Scotland, or the UK for that matter. To think one of our own would do it.'

'I didn't say the shooter was one of your own, sir. That's what I want to know, how skilled would you have to be?'

'Aye, well, let me see. If you were to get to the road that would be maybe seventy metres, the slipway somewhat less—maybe sixty to fifty metres. That's a reasonable distance. They shoot at seventy metres in the Olympics, but we have competitions that can range over one hundred metres so it's certainly very doable. And we are higher up here so the range will be a bit longer.'

'So, could you hit someone here with any guarantee?'

Jim looked at Hope with sad eyes, still struggling to come to terms with the idea that someone would use his beloved sport to try and kill a human being. Then he put his right arm up in front of him and bent his left arm placing the hand under the chin. He pivoted from his hips and then drew back his left hand in a motion that seemed to be the conclusion of an archery shot.

'I could definitely hit your target, Sergeant, but to guarantee hitting them in a place that would kill would be a struggle. It would take a particularly good archer to guarantee a kill.'

'Okay, that's helpful,' said Hope.

'Tell me, please, Sergeant, how were the people struck who

were hit? I mean, how did the arrow hit them? From what angle?'

'Well, from above.'

'But what angle? I mean there's above and then there's above?'

'How do you mean?' asked Hope.

'Well, you asked me if I could hit a person and yes, I could if I lined up as I did and fired the arrow directly to them. But that's not the only way to shoot an arrow. In the old days and in clout competitions these days, we shoot the arrow high and it comes down from the sky in a line much closer to the vertical. That would have a steeper angle of entry.'

'Hold on,' said Hope, 'I'm going to get our forensics expert here to discuss this with you.' Hope grabbed her mobile and called Mackintosh who advised she would be along directly. 'Jim, are both types of shooting as easy?' she asked the experienced archer.

'Easy? I'll be honest with you; it's been over fifty years and I still don't find this sport easy. Just obsessional.' The man laughed, a little uneasily, and then stared at Hope. 'If the arrows are coming in flat and not steep and he's hitting with regularity then he's definitely a decent archer. Not Olympic standard but a very good club archer. If they are raining down from above, then it's anyone's guess on their competence. How quick did they come?'

'Maybe ten seconds interval at most.'

'Well then, he's had a bit of practice. Let me get my bow.' Jim toddled off and came back with a silver case that was longer than it was fat. He proceeded to take out a set of curved bits of wood which looked like they were coated with plastic. These he attached to a black piece of metal that was long and had a handle in the middle of it. Next, he took out a long black piece of material and a string and proceeded to fix the string onto the pieces of wood, at either end causing the wood to bend backwards, and the bow took its final shape.

'Now that, Sergeant, is a basic recurve bow shape. If our man is using one of these, then in order to get the distance, he would need to be pulling anything from twenty-four to thirty-four pounds of limb.' Jim saw Hope's confused face. 'That's the curved bits of wood; limbs. They come with different poundage, or weight. Mine's a thirty-four-pound bow. Try and pull it but don't let go.'

Hope stood up to her full height and took the bow in her left hand. Jim stepped in and placed it in her right hand, telling her to draw the string back with her left. He gave her a piece of leather to place on the left hand over her fingers.

'The leather will keep the fingers safe,' he explained, and just pull back as best you can towards your chest, arms up straight like I had done previously.' Hope pulled the string and immediately felt a strain across her back. 'And hold it,' said Jim.

Hope held the bow for about three seconds then slowly let the tension off the string. 'Blimey, that's tough. How long do you hold that for?'

'About five to six seconds per shot. Shoot anything from eighty to one hundred and fifty shots in a session. So, you see, to fire that way you need to be practiced, simply to pull back the string repeatedly.'

Hope smiled at the man and saw Mackintosh appearing over his shoulder. 'Here's someone to help us, Jim, may I introduce Hazel Mackintosh, our senior forensic investigator on scene. Hazel,' said Hope, inviting Mackintosh to the conversation.

'This is Jim MacTavish. He's an expert in archery and has been helping me with trying to identify what sort of person would be required to carry out today's attack. Specifically, Jim wanted to know the angle of the arrows as they entered their targets.'

Mackintosh shook hands with Jim MacTavish and then took out a file. 'Now the teenager who was hit is a bit awkward as a test case as she was in the turn I think, so it's hard to be sure. But the child was sitting in a buggy when it hit her shoulder, so it would not have been vertical but would certainly be close to it.'

'Then he was not aiming at a specific person,' said Jim, 'or rather he was not shooting for a part of the body. He was dropping the arrows down on his target. Bit like the days of old where you drop the arrow onto a formation of pikemen or warriors, or even horsemen.'

'And that would mean what?' asked Hope.

'How far apart was the spread of arrows?' asked Jim.

'As far as we can tell from the marks on the ground, there's a spread over at least a thirty-metre radius, maybe further.'

'Then he's no expert, or he was not concerned with a single target. Did the description people gave of the bow say it had anything attached to it, like a long rod or that, at the front?'

'No,' said Hope, 'as I recall they spoke of the swept curves, like your bow.'

'No wheels at the top and bottom?'

'No.'

'Not a long single piece of wood?'

'No, why?'

'Just making sure that he was using a bow like mine. I think I may have said, it's a recurve bow. Do you have any of the

131

arrows?'

Mackintosh called to a man behind her and he came forward with two arrows in a clear evidence bag. Jim took it and began to look closely at it. He then held it in front of him and looked along the line of the arrow. On the end were fletches, in three colours.

'I doubt our man is an expert of any sort. Look at the fletches—that's the plastic feathers on the rear of the arrow. Not only are they of three different colours when they are normally two, but the amount of glue around the fletching makes it look like it's been done by a total amateur. Even the nocks and the tips are over glued. It's a right mess.'

'I'm confused,' said Mackintosh. 'I'm no expert, Jim, but don't you buy arrows complete?'

'You can do that,' nodded the man, 'but you don't have to. Some more advanced archers prefer to set their arrows up themselves to allow them to balance the arrows to the bow. But this guy has no idea what he's doing.'

'So why try?'

Hope saw Mackintosh's confused face but then something dawned on her. If Macleod was right, and that was still undetermined, then if you wanted to make each attack look different you could simply try another weapon. But then who was his target. But also, if you bought arrows then the colour of the fletches could give you away or at least narrow down who you were.

'Does this look like arrow glue, if there is such a thing?' asked Hope to Jim.

'I would not know. I couldn't tell one glue from another if it's all clear. But I will say this. The arrows are new. There's barely a dent in this one and the other has next-to-no markings on it.'

'Where can you get this kind of arrow?' asked Mackintosh.

'Online, archery shops, maybe even the big stores. It's an arrow that's at the low end. A proper arrow but certainly budget, a real beginner's arrow, not something an expert would use. Also, if the poundage of the bow was high, these are the wrong arrows. They wouldn't be stiff enough for a proper archer. I don't think this guy really understands his archery.'

Hope called Ross to her and thanked Jim MacTavish. The man passed his phone number to her and said he would be available at any time if she needed him. He then turned to Mackintosh and took her hand, shaking it politely.

'And may I say Hazel, it has been a particular delight. Excuse my rudeness but you seem a rather fine woman.'

As the archer walked away, Hope felt herself reeling a little from the comment until Ross interrupted her.

'Yes, boss.'

'Ross, get Stewart to start looking into orders from online stores in the local area. I want her to look for someone buying those arrows and the glue that's on them. Mackintosh will furnish you with the type of glue as soon as she can, if you would be so kind.'

Mackintosh was looking back down the bridge and at the retreating archer. Her face sported a beaming smile and her eyes seemed to be watering slightly.

'Mackintosh? Hazel? You okay?' asked Hope.

'Perfect, dear,' she replied, wiping her eyes with her sleeve. 'The glue, I'll get on it right away.' But Hazel Mackintosh's eyes still lingered on the man.

'Anything else come up from Stewart's investigations?' asked Hope.

'Not yet, but it's a lot of ground to cover so I doubt you'll see much fruit from it until a day or two from now. She was also running a lot of the interviews with me, so she's not been on it most of the day.'

'Good,' said Hope, 'tell her to burn the midnight oil on this one for me. Finding a link between targets is crucial if the boss is right about this being something personal.'

'Of course. By the way, I heard a rumour that up above are sending someone to help us. Parry's idea.'

Hope started. 'Who told you?'

'Heard a rumour from someone at Inverness station, one of the desk sergeants and you know how close to the rumour mill they are. Not sure you're going to like it though.'

'No!' Hope stood with both hands on her hips, her head shaking.

'Yes, so they say.'

'Over my dead body,' cried Hope and stormed off.

Ross turned to Mackintosh and shrugged his shoulders, but the woman was looking along the bridge. Ross checked her line of sight but the archer was now gone.

'Ma'am? Are you sure you're okay?'

Mackintosh nodded and smiled at Ross. 'A rather fine woman. I'll take that.' With that, she walked off leaving a bemused Ross standing on the bridge.

Chapter 16

Hope swallowed her last morsel of toast and threw a large gulp of coffee after it. The black liquid was Java, a particularly bitter-tasting coffee to Hope, but then again, everything today was going to be bitter. She had spent an hour on the telephone to DCI Dalwhinnie the previous evening stating that she was more than capable of handling things in the absence of Macleod and that she did not need another DS assisting her. What she meant, of course, was that she did not need Allinson, her previous lover, joining her team, especially as he had just gained the same rank as herself. But Dalwhinnie was insistent.

'I'm going to check out the archery leads Stewart came up with,' said Hope to Ross as they got set to leave the breakfast table. 'I'm sorry, Alan, but I need you to look after our hotshot arriving today. I know that's unfair on you, but I have a case to get on with and I don't need a nit-picking prig like that over my shoulder.'

Blimey, thought Ross, *things really did go sour.* Although he worked on the same murder team as Hope, Ross was not as privy to her private life as the Detective Inspector was, but he had heard about the bikini incident on that fateful holiday. Heck, everyone had.

'As you see fit, Hope. I don't mind; the case is what matters.'

'Did you get that from Macleod? It's the kind of thing he would say.' Hope placed her coffee cup away from her and stood up. 'I tried last night but didn't get him. Have you heard anything?'

'No, but Mackintosh spoke to him briefly. Jane is not in a good way, touch and go they say, possible bleeding on the brain. Currently in a coma.'

'Induced?' asked Hope.

Ross shook his head and then spied someone at the entrance to the hotel dining room. A tall figure entered, and Ross recognised the good looking Allinson. For once, Ross thought he saw what Hope had seen in the man but there was an element of caution in his thinking. Having been around Hope these last few months, it was hard for Ross not to see Allinson as a domineering arsehole, but then he only had Hope's word for it.

As Allinson approached, Ross went to get up from the table, but Hope put out a hand. 'You stay there, have another cup of coffee. I want to see him outside first of all. If you see Stewart, intercept her and wait for me here, Alan.'

Ross watched the two figures meet at the podium which held the breakfast list for the hotel, and he was impressed as Hope spoke not a word but merely pointed to the front of the hotel to Allinson. After the previous day where Hope had dressed in a somewhat smarter outfit than she normally wore, today the woman wore her black jeans, a white t-shirt and her leather jacket, a style Ross thought she kept for off-duty.

Wondering what to do as he waited, Ross felt his mobile vibrate and answered a call from a number simply labelled as 'Boss'. He felt a little apprehension placing the mobile to his lips and came up with the only word he could think of.

'Hello.'

'Ross, it's me, Macleod.'

'Sir, how is she?'

There was a cough down the line. 'Not good, Ross. But there's nothing to be done at the moment so I'm just sitting around the hospital cafeteria, drinking awful coffee and eating donuts like some American cop. Tell me what's happening.'

Ross relayed the events of the previous day to Macleod and waited in silence for his boss to say something.

'Is there anything else happening? I heard a rumour they were sending some assistance.'

'DS Allinson just arrived, sir.'

'Blast it, Ross, I told Dalwhinnie you didn't need anyone unless McGrath asked specifically.'

'Well, she's out there with him now. It seems heated.' Ross saw some pointed fingers outside the dining room window. Allinson seemed to be doing most of the lecturing but McGrath was standing firm, teeth gritted.

'Tell me, Ross, what's McGrath wearing?' Ross passed on the details. 'Good, she's being herself. Listen, Ross, I'm all right here. You guys have a job to do so don't be worrying about me. Mackintosh is being kept up to date so if you want to know how things are, just ask her. She knows that's how I want it. And don't tell McGrath I rang. She'll think I'm checking up on her, making sure she's all right.'

'Is that not what you're doing, sir?'

'Of course not, Ross. I'm merely looking out for a colleague and a friend. Just as I would for you or Stewart. Checking up is totally different.' There was a slight chuckle on the line. 'I'll go. But I'm here if you need me.'

Before Ross could say anything else the line went dead. There had been no offer of any thoughts on the developments. There had been no question of driving along Macleod's previous line of thought. He really had simply listened in.

Hope returned with Allinson and stood at the breakfast table, inviting Allinson to sit down. When he did, she continued to stand as she spotted Stewart in the distance. Waving her over, Hope briefed the team on today's actions, sending Allinson and Ross back to the scene to tie up with forensics and to see what other information could be dug up from the locals. Hope and Stewart would visit the list of archery suppliers she had found in the local area. That area stretched from Glasgow to Inverness so they would need to organise some uniforms to visit some of the sites.

As Hope dismissed the group, she told Ross to stay seated. When Allinson and Stewart had left the room, she spoke to him as he sipped more coffee.

'I've had a word with Allinson. Although he's technically your senior, I'm keeping you as my number two, Ross. This is basically because I don't trust why he's here, and he'll undercut me if he gets the chance. So, don't take any crap from him; you call the shots—understood? And if he doesn't like it, refer him to me. I'll handle him.'

'You okay, boss?'

Hope drew in her breath. 'Really, no, but if they are going to check me out then they are getting the full shebang and he can simply piss off.'

Ross almost laughed but he saw the fire in her eyes and decided it might not be the moment. Instead he thought he would try some encouragement.

'Well, you look the part. Your own style—looks great.'

'He bloody rang, didn't he? How is she?'

* * *

'That's a fifth possible supplier, Stewart, and we are nowhere. Dammit, we could use a break. There will be nothing from Glasgow either or they would be on the blower as fast as they could.' Hope stood beside the car and looked at her smaller colleague who did the only thing she ever did when the chips were down; she pushed her glasses back up her nose.

'There's a local guy selling out of his home address to try next. He's in Strontian, other side from the Corran ferry. There's been a transaction of arrows and glue on his Amazon sellers account to a local address, but it was listed as collection only. Worth checking.'

'Good, you drive, Stewart. I think I need to ponder some things.'

As they got into the car, Hope saw Stewart start to phrase a question, but then she declined.

'What is it?' asked Hope. 'Come on—spit it out. It's not the first time today you have tried to ask that question.'

'Well it's personal,' said Stewart. 'I shouldn't ask.'

'Kirsten, just ask; we're all girls if it's that personal.'

Stewart pushed the glasses up her nose as she pulled away in the car. 'They say he handed you back your bikini when you were on holiday. On a topless beach and all.'

'That he did.'

'I would have slapped him.' Stewart almost looked offended for Hope.

'And what makes you think I didn't?'

'You're too classy for that. I bet you just dropped the top in

139

the sand.'

Hope laughed out loud. 'No one knows that except Allinson and me. You really do get people, don't you?'

'Sorry. I wish I were like you. I would have just put on a t-shirt and stormed off. But then you have the figure.'

'I think you would turn heads too, Kirsten.'

And there it was. Hope could not remember a non-work conversation between them, and they had just had one about one of the most depressing times in Hope's life. Still, the sister was standing up for her so that was good. She should have known her colleagues would support her. Even Macleod had backed her decision even if he spoke of it in more reserved terms. It was her right to choose as he put it. When she had pressed him on whether he would have enjoyed it as a man, he had got very embarrassed.

Her mind drifted to him, sitting somewhere watching his loved one fighting for her life. He was older than her but there was a lot about Macleod that she loved and was frustrated by at the same time. On the odd occasion, she had even been envious of Jane, but that was just being foolish. Working together did these things to you.

It was over an hour later when they pulled up to a rather nondescript house set back from a neat road and a line of green, waving branches on a set of young trees. Stewart parked the car at the start of the small drive and Hope walked straight up and rapped with the large knocker sitting in the middle of the beige door.

'I'm coming,' said a voice, and then the door opened a few seconds later. A man in his thirties stood in a green t-shirt with a fantasy gaming logo across it. He wore lounge trousers, or pyjama bottoms as they used to be called, and Hope wondered if he had just risen.

'Sorry to disturb you, sir, I'm DS McGrath and this is DC Stewart. Are you James Maxwell?'

'Yes, yes I am,' said the man, smiling broadly as he took in the sight of the two detectives, to such a degree that Hope wondered if he had seen a woman before. James was slightly shorter than Hope and sported some stumble on his chin, but his hair was like a rug that had not been shampooed in a long time, or possibly never.

'Could we come in?'

James looked like he was about to wet himself at the thought, but he managed to open the door and ask them both to come inside. Hope stepped through and spun around as James asked, 'What's this about?'

'Just a little business transaction you were involved in, sir, nothing untoward on your part. We just need your help with some items you sold. I believe you sell archery equipment.'

James pointed to a door at the far end of the hallway they were in.

'That's the workroom and office. If you go in there, I'll have my records and you can look up what you need to.'

Hope was aware that the man's eyes followed both women everywhere and while he was extremely cordial and even somewhat old school in how often he seemed to open the door for them or pull out a seat, she felt just a little uneasy. When she entered the office, this feeling became even more so. One half of the space was dedicated to archery. There were pictures on the wall of the Olympics and people who must have been famous archers. Hope, however, could not name a single archer, never mind a particularly famous one. Well, maybe Robin Hood.

On the opposite wall were a number of large posters of fantasy figures. There were witches, dwarves, ogres, and dragons. Men stood in chainmail and women wore garments that defied their breath-taking figures. All Hope could think was that these women had stolen all the fixing tape the world could ever own. Either that or some wizard was casting a spell to keep their dignity in check.

'Mr Maxwell,' said Stewart, 'could you look up transaction number 2657ZW7G on your records and tell me about that order.'

'Of course, give me a moment. I'll need to switch on the computer. I was reading when you called. I have an afternoon that's screen free.'

As they waited for the system to load up, Hope stood and looked at the poster of a witch on the far wall. She got closer to it and realised that the woman had just a slip of clothing covering the bare essentials and that her backside was almost fully bare. The poster was obviously using a human model, although it may have been based on a cartoon image initially.

'Who wears stuff like this?' asked Hope.

James Maxwell went to speak but Stewart interrupted him. 'That's Alliah, witch of the seven veils of Castronian, keeper of the powerful amulet of Darfone, ghost in the night and mistress of the dark.'

Hope stared at Stewart who simply grinned. 'She's right,' said James, although that's a rather downplayed version of her outfit but then I doubt many women would wear it as daring as it was in the comic.'

'I did,' said Stewart. 'Comicon convention in Inverness. My friends dared me. It was February as well, bloody freezing.'

'I take it these were your wild school days,' asked Hope.

'No, two years ago.'

'Serious!'

'Yes, it's no different to you on a beach in the sun.'

Hope felt rebuked and looked a little ashamed until she noticed James Maxwell was simply staring at Stewart. 'Enough frivolity, Mr Maxwell, do you have that transaction for us?'

The man just smiled and then printed something out. Taking it over to Stewart he presented it to her, down on one knee and with his head hanging low, not daring to look at her. Hope looked over at Stewart.

'You dare not look at Alliah, lest she strike you down,' explained Stewart and then suddenly straightened on looking at the printout. Looking over at Hope, she simply nodded her head.

'Mr Maxwell, did you post this order?'

'No, ma'am, I don't post my archery orders unless I know who is getting them. This order was from an account that only had a pseudonym. He gave an address, but it had a different name attached to it when I looked it up. So, I said I was only happy for him to collect. An arrow is a lethal weapon in the wrong hands.'

'This man who collected the arrows, what height would you say he was?'

'Well, he was taller than yourself, witch Alliah but smaller than you, Sergeant. I'd guess five feet six, maybe five-seven.'

'I think you need to come with us, sir. Oh, and bring whatever glue you sell'

James Maxwell smiled and almost looked a little giddy.

Chapter 17

J ames Maxwell was sitting with a sketch artist in a room at the hotel in Fort William. He had given an address for his buyer whose name had simply been entered as 'Bowman' in the electronic log of the sale. The man had been very forthcoming about all of his dealings with the buyer and Hope was unsure if this was because he realised the trouble that had been caused with these arrows or if it was simply for Stewart who he had pestered with questions the whole way back to Fort William. It was hard to know if she was enjoying the attention or if she was simply keeping her informant interested. Surely, she could not be interested, thought Hope. But then again, he was being adoring and also a perfect gentleman.

Regardless of the man's designs or otherwise on Stewart, he had given the team a lead and Hope took Stewart away from her admirer to check out the address. She refrained at this time from informing Parry as all she had was someone with an approximate height. The glue they brought from the home shop was being sent to Mackintosh to see if there was a match to those in the arrows left at the scene. Hope's punt in the dark of matching arrows and glue to this attacker looked like it might work but she still had no proof at this time.

The address of 'Bowman' was in Glencoe, which was located

in a valley between several mountains, on the shores of Loch Leven. The house was on the outskirts of the village and was situated at the end of a long path beside a small wood. The whitewash which once may have shimmered in the light was now faded and covered with a multitude of dirty marks as if it had not been touched up in a decade or two. One windowpane was bordered up.

'What do you think?' Hope asked Stewart who was sitting in the passenger seat of the car. In the excitement, Hope had reverted to her role of driver as if Macleod were with her.

'Looks very run down, certainly not a family home, or one someone maintains. Might be a temporary abode. Whether he's here with the owner's permission is another question.'

'Let's see who's home,' said Hope, opening the car door, 'but be careful. If he's our killer, he might shoot first. Don't spook him if you can help it.'

Stewart nodded and together they approached the front door. It was flaking blue paint and a simple rap on the door caused it to swing open. Inside a fusty smell assaulted their noses.

'Hello, anyone home? This is the police. Is there anyone home we can speak to? Just a routine enquiry.'

Home stepped inside and found a damp hallway before entering the room immediately to her left. On a table in the middle of the room sat a rat, its long tail slicking out behind it, as it ate the remnants of a pizza.

'Shop-bought pizza,' said Stewart, 'I recognise it. Could be from any of the supermarkets or smaller outlets.' She reached over and shooed the rat from the table while Hope stood in the doorway in disgust at the animal fleeing. There were many fears in life that Hope had conquered but rats was one that stayed on the not-truly-vanquished shelf. Yes, she'd act if she needed to but if someone else was going to do it, then let them go at it.

Walking around the house, they found a toilet that had not be cleaned in eons, a kitchen with the gas connection removed and drawers in bedrooms that were empty. One of the beds showed a dip in it but whether it had been slept in, who knew. It might be an old impression.

'Mackintosh is going to thank you for this one,' said Stewart. 'I assume I'm making that call once we get outside.'

'Yes, absolutely,' said Hope, 'but tell her the glue is a priority. If it doesn't match, then this is all a waste of time.'

Once they had given the place a thorough going over, the pair stepped outside into the sunshine, grateful to be free of the smell of damp and decay. Hope wondered how anyone could sleep amidst that but maybe someone had. Maybe it was the perfect hideout if the owner thought it too dreadful to even visit.

'Any luck with tracing an owner of the property?' Hope asked Stewart, who consulted her phone.

'Apparently, it's a Mrs Agnes Robertson, also a Glencoe address. This is registered as a second home in her council tax paperwork.'

'Was the Inverness office digging that up for you?'

'Yes, young Ursula.'

'Good,' said Hope, 'keeps it off Glasgow's and Parry's desk until we want them to see it.'

It was an hour before Mackintosh and a small team arrived at the scene with a single uniformed officer. As the forensics chief stepped from her van, Hope watched her grimace as she stepped. Walking over to her, Hope offered a hand but was waved away.

'It's just some stitching from my operation,' said Mackintosh and looked at the building. 'Can we have some people murdered at the Ritz, or the Seychelles. Even a small spa in the country would be great.'

'Hold your nose in there, okay?'

Mackintosh laughed as her team walked on ahead of her and Hope grabbed the woman while she was on her own. 'Any word from Seoras?'

'Jane's still in a coma. They really don't think it's going to be good. Apparently, her body was battered so badly she has a multitude of broken bones. But it's the brain they are particularly worried about. She's in intensive care, watched round the clock.'

'How's Seoras?'

'How do you think?' blurted Mackintosh. 'I'd go to him but he wouldn't see that as appropriate, so he sits there alone. He has a sensitive side but he chooses to stand so aloof you can't help him.'

Hope noticed the tear in Mackintosh's eye. 'He confides in you more than most, Hazel. You're a good friend to him.'

'So why do I feel jealous of a woman fighting for her life? The woman walked through … , never mind. We have work to do.'

Hope grabbed Mackintosh's arm. 'I'm not Seoras but if you need to talk, I will listen.'

Mackintosh laughed. 'How would that work? He has more eyes for you than me.'

Hope let the woman's arm drop and then watched as she walked over to the house. In her mind she struggled to think that someone thought that she and Macleod could ever be anything but close professional partners. Yes, they had their moments, away from the public and they were just moments of close mutual support, nothing that truly overstepped a mark. How did the woman get to such a line of thought? Had Seoras said something when he was looking after her?

There was no time to wonder. A case was on the table and Hope needed to solve it. Shouting for Stewart, she got into the car but this time in the passenger seat. She needed some time to think.

In contrast to the damp, rat-infested house they had left, the abode of Mrs Agnes Robertson was that of a pretty, well-kept garden and a recently painted cottage. Knocking on the red door which had perfectly matching lintels, Hope stepped back and watched an older woman draw back the door. The woman was only five feet tall, smaller than even Stewart and with a frame that gave a new meaning to the word wiry. Her white hair, however, was perfectly brushed and although lacking body, was stuck fast in position. *Probably a can of mousse on it,* thought Hope.

'Mrs Robertson? I'm DS McGrath and this is DC Stewart. We're here to ask about your other home, at the other end of the village.'

'Is it all right?' the woman interrupted.

'There's not been a fire or anything, ma'am but has it been occupied recently?'

The woman's face became as white as her hair. 'No, Hamish has been dead six years and I haven't touched it. I can't bear to go in. My nephew took away all the clothes not long after it happened—they went to the charity shop. It would have been a sin not for someone to get the benefit. But I haven't stepped inside in over four years. Why, tell me, why do you ask?'

'It has been linked to an investigation we are running, ma'am. Not to any wrongdoing on your side. It appears someone has been using the house. But I believe they are gone now.'

After stepping inside with the woman for ten minutes and making sure she would recover from this strange news, Hope strode back to the car. 'Bloody missed him, Stewart. Dammit, missed him. We were so close.'

'If he's the one. We've no proof.'

'True, but he is. I think the boss was right. It feels amateur and yet he covers up a lot of things. He didn't panic when James Maxwell refused to post the arrows. Just popped over.'

'But we don't know where he is. If we get the sketch, then we could go public, show it on the telly and ask for any identification from the masses.'

'I'd have to run that upstairs as they might not want the panic being spread. That's been one bonus about having them over the top. The press has not been after me for a statement.'

Stewart looked at the mobile in her hand and then told Hope she had to take the call. As her colleague turned away, Hope's own mobile rang.

'Sergeant, it's Allinson. I was just looking for an update on what's happening if that's all right.'

Hope cursed in her head. He was being very formal and by the book, but she knew he was simply checking up on her. Hope relayed the events of the day in a systematic fashion with little emotion before asking how the scene at Ballachulish Bridge was.

'We are just about done but you were a bit premature taking Mackintosh away from here. Jona Nakamura was looking for an update and one of the juniors had to give it. She wasn't best pleased as I had to fill in some blanks for her.'

149

'I think Jona can handle it, and if she can't she has my direct line; thank you, Sergeant. We may need to go public with our sketch from Mr Maxwell today. Can you give thought to the proper media channels? Take a bit of work off Ross.'

Hope heard Allinson groan. 'You know I can do all that for you, take over Ross' work. Then you'd have your lackey to run your errands and my competent hands to help guide you along. Feels like you are winging this, Hope.'

'It's DS McGrath to you, and I am the senior officer here; they gave me the role, not you. You're just here to help and no doubt run your little thoughts back to Parry and his cronies. Just get on with what I ask.'

'This is going to blow up in your face, Hope. You can't follow an old man's gut when it's clear to everyone else there's a terrorist group acting here. I'm only trying to protect you.'

'Own me is what you wanted. Get your job done, Allinson.'

Parry and his cronies, did I seriously just say that? I mean I couldn't care less what I call Allinson, but I need to be careful around Parry.

'Boss?'

Hope looked around to see Stewart standing looking at her questioningly. 'Yes?'

'I just said to you, "I had a rather interesting phone call." But you seemed distracted.'

'Yes, I was.' Hope had no intention of explaining. 'What's the call about?'

'You know when I went to Glasgow to follow up on the gun? Well, that was Paddy Smythe, contact of the boss. He says he has some more information but this time about something larger.'

'Larger than a gun?'

'Wants to see us, now.'

Hope had never met Macleod's elusive contact, but she was too busy. 'Okay, grab a car and go see him. Let me know what he has.'

'No, boss, he asked specifically for you. Said he tried Macleod, but he didn't answer. He doesn't have your number, but he has mine. He said there were lives at stake.'

There are always bloody lives at stake, thought Hope. 'Where?'

'Bridge of Orchy station. He's on his way up by train. We have an hour before he gets here.'

'Great. Then let's get some food. I'm starved.'

An hour later, Hope stood on the platform of the small station at Bridge of Orchy. The stony mix of pebbles on the platform seemed unusual to Hope but the white waiting room building gave a quaint look to what was a modernised country platform. Everywhere, the purple Scotrail branding could be seen and as the diesel train pulled up, only three carriages long, Hope felt herself becoming intrigued. Stewart was excited but she was fighting to stay calm, evidenced by her constant agitation of her glasses.

Only one person stepped off the train and he was wearing a brown sports jacket and a baseball cap. Stewart strode forward to the one-armed man and shook his hand vigorously.

'Paddy, good to see you.'

The man smiled and then with a harsh northern Irish accent replied, 'You too, Kirsten. A pleasure. And this must be your boss, the free-spirited Hope McGrath. Good day to you, Sergeant.'

Hope was unsure how to take this greeting. 'Good day, Mr Smythe. It seems you know a lot about me.'

'I know a lot about anyone I deal with—comes with the

territory. As you are Macleod's number two, I needed to know you were reliable if we had to come at things from different angles. Turns out you are rather like an associate of mine. I bet you scare the living daylights out of them when they see you coming. Dogged, just like my Susan. Clever man, your boss.'

Hope was again wrong footed and simply smiled. The man was charming if somewhat unnerving. 'What have you got for me, Mr Smythe?'

'Paddy, please, and once the train has gone.'

The three of them stood in silence as the train departed, leaving them alone on the platform. Hope went to speak but Paddy held up his hand.

'Listen, I've been keeping an eye on the gun runners who sold the weapon used in the Fort William shootings. It was by chance that while watching one of them, I found them pressurising another dealer about our mutual friend. Apparently, this dealer sold an item to the man around the same time as our gun dealers did. The problem is this weapon is somewhat large. It's a small rocket launcher.'

'What?' Hope blurted out.

'Exactly. Not too big, so he can carry it about with him, reasonably easily in a car, or even in a bag over the shoulder if he wants. It's dangerous enough to take out people. I think he only has the one missile, but I cannot be sure. You need to get an ID on this man and fast, Sergeant. I'll keep pushing my end but to be honest the trail is pretty cold now. These dealers don't keep contacts especially if the heat is on about what they have just sold.'

'So where do we start in tracing this item?' asked Hope.

'You won't but this is coming. So, you need to get him sooner rather than later.'

'But it's the same man?'

'Definitely. New player too, possibly a novice but they are saying well read. Knows terms and that but not used to playing with the big guys.'

'How do I reach you if I need you again, Mr Smythe?'

'You won't,' smiled the Ulsterman. 'But Macleod has my number. Not looking good for his partner though. Let's hope she pulls through.'

With that Smythe walked to the waiting room and promptly lay down on the bench at one side, apparently trying to go to sleep. Hope stood and digested what had been said. *A rocket launcher? Where was he looking to attack now?*

Chapter 18

The meeting had been hastily convened and had not been requested by Hope. She sat on her seat staring at the telephone as the conference call continued. Parry had some news for everyone. The terrorist branch had a suspect under surveillance and they were convinced this was their man. Apparently, all the motives were satisfied; a disaffected Irishman and former member of a small dissident republican fringe branch who had recently been out of the country and probably training. He was in the Glasgow area but had taken to disappearing to the countryside recently. His anger at the invading British had never subsided but he also had racist tendencies.

Hope had waited for the initial clamour and pride of Parry to subside before she interjected with her thoughts on the archer she was tracing. She also added a word from her 'source', saying how they had been accurate about the gun and now they believed a rocket launcher had been purchased. Parry had been dismissive, saying Hope was chasing a copycat with her archer and that the lead to the dissident Irishman was more solid as he had connections with Seamus Finney, the suspect found with the Semtex explosives. After a protest, Hope stayed quiet as her voice was not being heard.

'So, McGrath, I want you to continue on the trail of that copycat attacker as we need to put a lid on that sort of thing, make potential wannabies aware that we shut them down with force. You've done great work, especially with Macleod missing. So, stick to it.'

Hope picked up a paper cup from her desk and hurled it at a bin on the other side of the room. It missed lamentably and she found herself swearing at Parry. It was a good job she had the mute button on or he might have been rather put out. As the call ended, DCI Dalwhinnie asked Hope to remain on the call at the end so she could talk to her.

'McGrath, I want to echo Parry's words. You have done a great job in the absence of Macleod, a job he told me you would do. But now you need to end the lines of enquiry Macleod was chasing and leave the terrorist incidents to the Branch set up for them. You are to solely concentrate on getting this copycat attacker and then get back to Inverness and get on with your regular policing. You can have Macintosh if you need her as I think Miss Nakamura will be greatly occupied in the days to come.'

There was silence on the line. 'Did you hear me, Sergeant?'

'Yes, ma'am.'

'You seem to be saying very little.'

'Well I happen to disagree totally with the decisions being made. I think Mr Parry is overplaying his cards. I don't think he has much more than we do and is going on instinct that it's a terrorist. My boss's instincts were different, and I have to admit on disagreeing with him initially but the more I have seen of this case, the more I see his point. It all feels very personal and amateurish.'

'But you have no suspect, merely a sketch picture of a man

155

who bought arrows and glue. At best, you have the copycat attacker, but nothing to the real attacks. And your inference about a rocket attacker is not very productive. It's not even a registered source, just a common link to the underworld.'

Hope wondered how Patrick Smythe would enjoy being called a 'common link to the underworld'. Maybe he would as he did not seem too bothered with precedent.

'But we have a gut feeling ma'am. One that I didn't have but now, I feel it, too.'

'It's admirable,' continued Dalwhinnie, 'that you would want to hold up your boss's name at a time when he is under so much pressure. But I think you are letting a little too much personal judgment come into this. Get your copycat attacker and get back to Inverness, Sergeant, that's an order.'

'Yes ma'am,' said Hope and abruptly cancelled the call. *Hold up your boss's name. Personal judgement.* 'Allinson!' yelled Hope to the door of her room. 'Get your backside in here!'

The door opened calmly and Allinson walked in as if no one had been shouting at all.

'You contemptuous little shit!'

'That's highly unprofessional,' said Allinson.

'Been crying to mother, have we? Did she send you as a spy or did you just volunteer your opinion? I can't believe you did that, go behind my back. And don't deny it. From what she said it's bloody obvious.'

'I was only trying to protect you, Hope. I didn't want to see you throw your career down the pan.'

Hope strode around her desk and placed a finger on Allinson's chest. 'Don't even pretend that you care for me. All you want is a pretty little obedient woman on your arm. Well, that boat sailed when you couldn't handle a proper woman.

As for watching my back, I have someone for that. He's sat in there and Ross is twice the partner you could ever be.'

Allinson tilted his head back, nose in the air. 'Oh, I see; like that, is it. A close working relationship now the old man's gone.'

'He's gay, you ignorant arse. I was speaking professionally.'

Hope held her stare but deep in her stomach she found herself struggling not to laugh at Allinson's face at the revelation of Ross' sexuality.

'You could never take advice,' said Allinson after a time.

'We are no longer chasing terrorists, just a copycat attacker so I think all your help is no longer needed. Go back to Inverness and your own department. And keep out of my life.'

Allinson strode out with a hurt look on his face and Hope collapsed in her seat. After a moment she began to laugh, heartily, and then she cried whilst laughing. *How the hell do I pick them?*

The door was knocked and then it opened to reveal Ross juking his head in. 'Everything okay, boss?'

'Come in, Alan, come on in. Do you know that I have just been accused of having an affair at work with you?'

Ross look at Hope awkwardly and then seemed to be searching for a hidden bottle or a needle, perhaps.

'I'm perfectly sober. Allinson has been spying on us for upstairs and I have just given him the heave-ho. He tried to say I was sleeping with you.'

Ross looked a little embarrassed. 'Well, you're not my type' boss' as you know but you might have been preferable to him. What did you … Sorry.'

'What did I see in him? A hulky body and he does have good

eyes. But he wasn't such an arse then. Anyway, we need to step things up. I'm going to ring Macleod for a little direction. Has Stewart come up with anything on the victims?'

Ross turned to the door and shouted for Stewart. The woman came rushing in and stood before Hope with a few papers in her hand. 'The boss wants to know what you have, Stewart,' said Ross.

'Okay, well, it's a real mixed bag. I have Germans and other tourists to begin but then we have two NHS workers in the last two attackers, both on different tiers but I think they worked in a similar place, at least for a little while. I'm still looking into that. Our photofit is going out to local news this evening. I believe the senior teams have already informed the press that the Ballachulish Bridge attack was a copycat affair. I take it we are not of that opinion.' Stewart looked at her two bosses who both nodded their heads.

'Oh, and Mackintosh has confirmed the arrows and the glue were both bought by our mystery purchaser from Mr Maxwell.'

'Was he still about earlier?' asked Hope.

'Yes, he waited for me for three hours to give me an Alliah playing card. Was extremely sweet of him.'

'Indeed,' said Hope, 'just don't let it get in the way.' *Like I can talk about relationships and work*, she thought. 'Okay give me the room; I need to talk to the boss. Good work the pair of you but get me an ID on that buyer.'

With the junior pair gone, Hope poured herself a cup of coffee and sat down on her chair, placing her feet on the desk in front of her. As she rang Macleod's mobile, she gulped down the hot liquid and wondered if she was wise calling him. Then he answered and she had made her choice.

'Seoras, how are things?'

'Not good. They think she may be bleeding on the brain and she's gone to theatre. I don't know how long she's going to be in there. It's so bloody useless being here. The doctors have things to do, the nurses too, even the porters run from here to there, but I just sit and wait. I just pray she'll pull through.'

'At least you have your God,' said Hope. 'It must be good to have a faith at these times.'

'Really? He's on mute for some reason. The two times in my life when I have been ripped apart and He goes on mute. There's no guarantees, Hope; did you know that? Prayer, it doesn't answer everything. Prayer works, they say. Do they even have a clue what they are saying? He's as much a mystery to me at these times as he is to you, Hope. But you called with a question. What do you need?'

Hope shrunk in her chair. How could she bother him at a time as this? How insensitive was she becoming? 'It's fine, Seoras, you got a lot on.'

'Shut up and ask what you wanted to ask. Yes, I have a lot on, whatever that means, but I can do nothing about it. So, tell me what you need to know and maybe it'll take my mind off this constant fretting. It's not like I can change anything. So, what is it?'

Hope relayed the events of the case to Macleod and could hear him grunting down the telephone at Parry's decisions and then exclaiming out loud at Dalwhinnie's actions.

'I walked the beat with Dalwhinnie in Glasgow. Saved her from a kicking one night and took a punch to my ribs that broke one. Also punched an over amorous Sergeant for her. I thought she would be a little more willing to give you a freer leash. I recommended she leave you alone. Sorry about Allinson, that's just rubbish. You didn't need that but good for you sticking it on him.'

'So, what do I do, Seoras? Do I simply give this up and head home once we do our duty here? Or do I push through the lines of enquiry further? Keep going despite what I've been told?'

Hope heard a Tannoy in the background and thought Macleod seemed to be getting up and walking.'

'I'm going to walk her to theatre, Hope, so I haven't got time. It's your case, your decision. You know what I would do, you've worked with this awkward bugger long enough now. But it's your decision and your case.'

'Yes, sir. Hope it goes well, Seoras. Anything I can do for you?'

'Pray, Hope, pray your guts out for her.'

'But you said He was quiet, and there were no guarantees.'

She heard Macleod laugh. 'What else do I have? It's why they call it faith, Hope.'

She smirked. He was no standard Lewis man when it came to his faith. 'All the best, sir.'

'Oh, Hope. Now you're going to chase this through, make sure you push Smythe to dig deep for you. He's a little on the shady side of operations but he's a good guy.'

'Yes, sir. I'll pray!' With that Hope put the telephone down. *Hang on*, she thought, *I never said I was going to chase this down. I am, but I never said. He knows me too well.*

Chapter 19

J udy Finnieston pulled up the sock that came out of the top of her hiking boot and pulled it tight. She had broken the pair of boots in the previous week on a small trek, but she hoped she really looked the part today. After all, Sam was trekking with the party today.

It was a bit of a come-down, in reality, but the man was so sweet. Judy was his senior by ten years but in the office that never seemed to matter as she caught his eye several times. Not only was Sam younger but he was also many levels below Judy in the hierarchy at the department. But after her rather acrimonious split from a chance lover she had met over a year ago, Judy was keen to get back in the game. The man had wanted to know all about her business and her past and then had seemed to become more and more angry and abusive to her. That sort of attitude was not acceptable. She was turning forty soon and if she wanted that family she would need to move quickly.

Although only nine in the morning, there was a warmth to the air that was impressive for a Scottish summer. The recent good weather had brought out people in their thousands to the Highlands and Judy tried hard not to get annoyed by the tourists. Instead she looked across to the Lycra trousers of

Sam. Now that was a butt to get hold of.

After a moment's thought about whether to put on her fleece, she decided to go for broke and wrap it around her waist, leaving only her sweat-controlling t-shirt on and wandered over to join the rest of the party. They were at the Water of Nevis, in the shadow of the mountain itself, here to take a walk through the valley and in Judy's case, to get a certain man alone and engage him so he could not get away. She could smell the dew leaving the ground and heard the laughter of work colleagues. Everything seemed right, despite the six o'clock start. *Play it right, Judy, and he'll still be with you at six o'clock tomorrow morning.*

Whilst everyone was getting out of their cars and adjusting their gear for the day, Judy took a moment to look around and spied a rather strange figure along the road. There was only one way in until you reached the car park and this person, dressed in a red hoodie and camouflage trousers, was standing there with a number of car horns beeping behind him. Windows were being wound down and verbal abuse had begun for this idiot on the road.

The man had a large backpack over his shoulder which he now placed on the ground. Judy watched him unzip the bag, kneel, and reach inside it. As he stood up, she realised he had something in both hands, like a large tube of some sort. Then she spotted the red at the front of the apparatus. Something clicked in her head. Didn't the news say something about that gunman wearing a hoodie.

Someone was getting out of the car behind the man but then she saw that driver turn and run. The man holding the tube had it pointing her direction. Surely this was a bit of laugh. She looked across at the rest of her gathered party, but they looked anxious.

'That's a rocket launcher. He's got a rocket launcher!' shouted Sam.

Judy felt a chill race up her spine and started to spin this way and that, looking for cover. Where do you hide from a rocket? Her legs felt like jelly, as if she were about to collapse but she manged to get herself to the far side of her car and ducked down behind it. Yells and scream filled the air but there had been no sound of a rocket being fired. Maybe it was all a hoax, some cruel prank or someone wanting to get on the news. A cry for help—that would be it.

Turning around, her back no longer to the car, Judy peered over the top of the car's side, through the windows and saw the figure still standing there. There was a flash of fire from the tube and the rocket started flying towards her car.

***

Hope placed the telephone on the receiver and sat back into her seat. It felt strange going behind the DCI's back but in truth, what choice did she have? In her mind, Hope knew that she was chasing no copycat. Yes, she would pretend she was for the record but involving Patrick Smythe to the level she had asked him to investigate was no simple measure. This was no retreat to Inverness.

Smythe had heard rumours about a rocket launcher but Hope wanted the rumour confirmed and traced as best as the man could. It was an underground scene that for Hope to enter would have involved other departments and there was no way she could run that past the DCI. So, she asked Smythe to get involved more deeply. She was unsure if Macleod would have approved but he did use Smythe at times, did he not? Thankfully Stewart had a number, so she didn't need to ask Macleod.

A rap was heard on the door and a tired looking Stewart entered. It may have been the first part of the day but Stewart looked like she had not seen her bed. The hair was tied up but several strands were lying loose and Stewart was still wearing a fleece, something she liked to do when she worked later hours.

'Boss, I think I may have a link between two of our victims: Peter Chen who died on the ferry, and Martin Doonan, although he obviously survived but he could have been the target. I said before that there were two NHS people on our list; well, it seems they have actually worked together on several committees which make executive decisions. I can't see anything that is particularly contentious yet, but it might be something for someone to have a grievance about.'

'Good work!' said Hope, 'but keep digging. I don't see how the German tourists were a target. Macleod floated the idea of practice but surely you would just take a gun out to a field and shoot things.'

'Maybe, but how do you practice with a bomb?' asked Stewart. 'If the boss is right and this is a solo effort because of some agenda, then we have to think differently. It's not an expert we're up against although they do seem well read. After all, they are handling these weapons, albeit inexpertly.'

'True. Hopefully, we can get something back from our photofit. Anyway, we have Mr Smythe looking into the rumours for us. You have to hand it to our attacker; he's left truly little around for us to find. No markings or fingerprints on the arrows. If he hadn't used the glue on the arrows from the same order, we would have no idea about him. Mackintosh found nothing in the house except some DNA, but it has no match on record. I guess that backs the boss's theory this is personal, someone not used to carrying out these sorts of actions.'

'I'll get back on this, see what more I can find about these two NHS figures. I'll also speak again to Martin Doonan, see if he can shed some light.' Stewart took off her glasses and cleaned them. 'If these people were the targets, then why the bomb and the gun shootings. He used a crossbow and a bow and arrow. If the first two were a practice, then do we expect to see another bomb, or a shooting?'

'I don't know,' said Hope, 'but there's nothing to say if the person will stop. If we knew the agenda, we'll have more to go on. Find me that agenda, Stewart.'

'Sir.' Placing her glasses back on, Stewart exited the room and Hope wondered if she was pushing the girl too hard. It was a lot to be the one trying to unlock a secret while everyone around was being shot or bombed.

Hope walked to the coffee machine on the desk at the side of the room and poured herself another cup. As she did, she heard someone outside bursting through the outer doors. Her heart skipped a beat as she waited for the person to enter. It was like this every time there was an attack—the news being raced to the investigator in charge. And she felt this piece of horror coming towards her.

Ross burst into the room. 'Ben Nevis Water, sir, he's used the rocket launcher. Multiple wounded and at least two dead.'

'Damn! Get the car, Ross. It won't be ours to deal with, but we need to go there. Stewart stays and finds me that link. I'll be outside with you in two minutes.'

Hope heard Ross leave the room and then slurped down her

coffee quickly. *Parry will be all over this, but I said about the rocket launcher. I'll need to be cool about that, try not to gloat but get whatever information I can. I wonder what his target was up to when this happened. Maybe they will believe our theory now.*

The drive to Ben Nevis Water was not long from Fort William but the road as they got closer was full of emergency vehicles and dazed tourists. They had to park up a half a mile away and walk the last part to the attack site and Hope found herself almost running along.

By her reckoning, the attack had taken place about an hour previously and Hope knew that there would be search efforts underway but there were no cameras around, no CCTV to record the incident. She checked in with the Sergeant looking after the scene and then saw Parry in the distance. Calmly, she approached him.

'McGrath, looks like our man has struck again. He's a right Irish devil. We have two dead here and at least seven injured and lot of people in shock.' Parry looked around and seemed a little exasperated.

'I thought you had the Irishman under surveillance?'

'He broke off from our tail. Lost him last night. But from a mobile phone image I have seen, it certainly looks like him. Hard to believe he managed all these attacks, except the bomb at Skye, of course. He got a ringer to plant that. He's the perfect height for the footage we have. I suspect he has an old armoury somewhere.'

'But what about the rumour of the rocket launcher? It could be recent.'

'Just an unsubstantiated rumour; you know I need more than that. Anyway, don't get in the way but if you want to help with the interviewing of the onlookers, feel free. It's all a bit chaotic and I need the uniforms and other troops on a search for him. So please, take care of the initial interviews and feed me anything important.' Parry turned away as a mobile was handed to him.

Hope felt the anger building up in her. *Bloody surveillance people.* But there was nothing else to do and she could easily be kicked off the scene, so she told Ross what Parry had said and began to co-ordinate with the on-scene Sergeant about interviewing the onlookers.

Back along the road, a small unit of police officers were keeping those present at the attack together outside an on-scene incident hut that had recently arrived. Officers were taking names and details but not interviewing them so to speak. Hope asked for a list of the people present and then asked that they be sent into the hut one by one, so initial statements could be taken.

It took Hope and Ross a few hours to go through everyone's statement. The on-scene Sergeant had sent a local CID detective to take the statements of anyone in hospital who was up to the task. One of Hope's last interviewees, named Blossom, was a child of maybe six. As she was brought into the room with a female constable, Hope saw how frightened she was. The constable advised that the child's mother had been hit in the attack and was in hospital—not critical, but seriously injured.

'Hi,' said Hope. 'My name is Hope and I'm a police detective.'

The child, a young girl with long blonde hair, looked at her in confusion. 'You're not a police person. She's a police person.' The girl pointed at the constable with her. 'You're wearing a t-shirt and jeans. Police people wear uniforms.'

Hope laughed at the simple deductions being made but could

see the girl was also afraid. 'Your mum has gone to hospital, you know that?' The girl nodded. 'Well' we can get you to her or your dad very soon.'

'I don't have a dad. Never had one. Everyone else in school has one.'

Hope was beginning to feel a little out of her depth. 'Okay, that's fine.'

'No, it's not. Means I'm weird. They all say you have to have a dad at school, and I don't cos I'm weird.'

'Well, people think I'm weird,' replied Hope. 'I'm a weird policewoman because I don't wear a uniform. So, we can be weird together, if that's okay?' The girl looked at Hope with questioning eyes and then looked up and down at her, taking in the T-shirt and jeans.

'I like your boots,' she said suddenly and again Hope struggled not to laugh.

'I need you to tell me what you saw,' she asked the girl.

'No.'

'It's okay; you can tell me.'

'No.'

'Why? What's the matter?'

Blossom looked at Hope and had tears running from her eyes. 'I don't want to see that again. I don't want to look again.'

'Did you get hurt?' asked Hope, knowing the child only had scratches.

'No, because Mum protected me. She threw me.'

'Okay, instead of seeing that, did you see the man who did this?'

'Yes, he walked past me, looked at me. He had a hood on.'

Hope tried not to seem too eager and scare the child. 'Did you see his face?'

'Yes. He had a big nose. Big eyebrows too.'

'What about his mouth?'

'He had a snoodie around that. I think they are called snoodies. His was black.'

'Do you think if I got someone who draws in here you could tell the person what the man looked like?'

'I can draw him. Get me a crayon.'

Hope smiled at the child and wondered how best to get the information she needed from her. 'Okay we'll get you some crayons and then we'll get my friend and you can draw together.'

An hour later, Hope was looking at a sketch done by the artist. It showed a man with bushy eyebrows and a rather pronounced nose. In her other hand was a stickman who held a stick with fire coming out of it. In reality, Hope wondered if either drawing showed enough detail to be useful. The man in the artist's picture was very non-descript. But she knew she had to show what she had come up with to Parry. There was little else. The man had appeared as if from nowhere and then after firing had fled into the countryside.

But one point had been made by several of the interviewees; the man had targeted a woman and then the car she was behind. The car in question was obliterated and they were still finding parts of the woman. From others who had gathered to walk with the victim, Hope found out she was Judy Finnieston, a senior finance officer in the NHS. She had instructed Ross to get the information to Stewart immediately.

Parry dropped by the mobile hut in quite a flap. 'You have something for me, Sergeant. Tell me you have something because this bugger's as elusive a bastard as I have ever known.'

'Well he was wearing the hoodie as per most of the other

attacks and was the same build and height. However, a child did see him as he went by her. My guess is he may have stopped to say sorry as her mother was seriously injured.'

'I doubt that; our suspect is a cold one.'

Hope raged in her mind. *That's because it's not him!* 'I do have a sketch of his eyes and eyebrows.' Hope passed the sketch to Parry.

'Not especially useful really but it could be our man. But there was nothing else?'

'No, sir. It would appear he's getting better at this.' But the comment was lost on Parry as he raced off to a waiting Sergeant. Turning to Ross, as ever by her side, Hope pointed to the car.

'Well, we did our bit for them. We'll see if the Sergeant wants anything more from us and then let's get these statements filed. After that we can get back on our man and find him.'

'By the sounds of it, he's on the run out in the country,' said Ross.

'No, Ross, he'll have not had too far to go. This is a local man; I'm sure of it.'

Chapter 20

As they drove back to Fort William in the car, Hope had a thought. Parry was up to his neck looking for the suspected fugitive but really, she should go on a different tack. The woman who died, Judy Finnieston, would have a workplace and possibly they might know some of the more controversial items she had to deal with. There could be something in there that someone would object to or maybe they had been hurt by a decision she had made. Given that she was quite high up the ladder in the management team, she would sign off on a lot of issues but at least it might give more guidance to Stewart on what to look for.

'Stewart,' said Hope, having called her junior colleague, 'can you get me an address for the secretary or work partner of Judy Finnieston? She's in finance in the NHS and was one of the victims at the rocket site. She probably works in Glasgow but I believe her colleagues were up here with her on a walking trip so someone might live out this way. Can you get a name for the best person to talk to?'

'Sure,' said Stewart, 'but I wouldn't come back here to Fort William. If a lot of her colleagues were out walking with her, the person you need will probably still be there. I'll try and identify the best person to talk to.'

Hope told Ross to pull over while she awaited Stewart's response. Of course, Stewart was right; the best people were probably with her on this walk, but you never knew. After ten minutes, Stewart called back quoting a Leslie Anderson as her secretary. Hope didn't recognise the name as someone she had interviewed and held the name up in front of Ross.

'Young woman, I interviewed her. She was out of the way at the back of the group and was relatively unscathed. She was noticeably quiet.'

'No wonder, having seen her boss die. She might still be there if she's needing to get home. Maybe her car was affected by the blast. Anyway, turn around and we'll find out, but we go in as having thought about something in her statement if anyone asks, looking for a little clarification. Until we can get a name, we don't want to rock the boat, or we'll be hightailing it back to Inverness.'

As they returned to the attack site, the road was no less busy than when they had arrived. But there were fewer ambulances which had been replaced by a number of forensic team vehicles. As Hope checked in with the Sergeant overlooking the scene, she saw Jona Nakamura in the distance, wearing her white coverall and looking a little pale. The constant effort of charging around sites and being pressured for some tell-tale clue must be taking its toll. Mackintosh was hovering behind Jona and on seeing Hope, she broke off and came towards her.

'How goes it, Sergeant?'

'In truth, not well. I still think Parry is on the wrong path but, although we matched up our guy to the arrows and glue, we haven't had a hit from the publicity. Can't believe the DNA didn't match anyone.'

'Well,' said Mackintosh, 'that might be because you are on

172

the right lines. Someone who has their own reason for doing this, and it would have to be extreme—may not be someone who broke the law previously. Other than the arrows, we don't have direct DNA for any implements used in the attacks and as Parry believes that was a copycat, we have nothing to rule out his Irishman. Hence, we are seeking every bit of the rocket we can find. Mind you, that will be an absolute trawl given how it blew up into a million pieces. Keep going, Sergeant McGrath. Seoras would.'

Hope nodded but inside she was not happy at being compared to Macleod. She was her own woman. No, who was she kidding? After working with him for so long, she was bound to be picking up on his ways and thoughts.

Ross took Hope into the interview hut they had used before where he had brought Leslie Anderson who had been waiting for a taxi. As they sat down in a couple of plastic chairs, the woman looked nervous.

'It's okay, Miss Anderson; these are just some routine questions which we need to clarify some questions for us about why Mrs Finnieston was attacked. I believe she was a finance executive in the NHS and you were her secretary. Can you tell us what level of projects or work she would sign off on?'

The woman was red-eyed and stared at the rather drab wall behind Hope. 'I really just want to go home. I want to look for a large bottle of wine and then drink it. All of us are talking about it. How do you unsee that?'

'You don't, Miss Anderson, but you may yet come to learn to live with it. I was asking what sort of level within the NHS Mrs Finnieston signed off work for.'

The woman shifted in her seat and tried not to look Hope in the eye. Ross put his hand across the table in a gentle fashion.

'Mrs Anderson? Leslie, please, this is important. We realise you've experienced something shocking, but we need to do this or else we may have another incident like this on our hands. We can't afford that. So please, do your best to answer the questions and we shall get you home as soon as we can. Your help is greatly appreciated.'

Leslie Anderson sniffed and then smiled at Ross. 'Of course,' she said.

How does Ross do that? thought Hope. *He's so good with people, gentle when he needs to be giving that little push, firm, but with compassion.*

'Mrs Finnieston,' started Leslie Anderson, 'is a senior executive for the Borders and West Region of the NHS and as such, puts her signature to nearly all projects from a finance point of view. Her team investigates and cooperates on the larger projects and also assists with funding options.'

'Has there been any controversial projects in recent times that you remember, Mrs Anderson, ones that may have caused Mrs Finnieston some difficulty?' Ross spoke with an even and delicate tone which Hope marvelled at and she saw their interviewee try to recall some of the past years with her boss.

'Mrs Finnieston, Judy, was tough but she was also very conscientious. A lot of the projects are controversial to one person or another but none of that ever seemed to bother her. She was passionate at times, especially about cancer funding but I only ever saw her under pressure once.'

'And when was that?' asked Ross.

'About two years ago. There was an application to add a new leukaemia drug to the list. It had passed all the regulation checks; it was only the funding that was holding up the implementation of this drug, but it seemed to me that things

174

went from full steam ahead to a complete halt overnight. I remember Mrs Finnieston getting a call just before I left the office late. It seemed to bother her, so I did what a good secretary does; I waited until the call was finished, gave her a moment, and then went to see if she was all right.'

'And was she?'

'No, not at all. She was seething but there were tears in her eyes, too.'

Ross leaned forward again. 'Did you understand why it was getting to her so much?'

'Well, at first, I thought she was just thinking of the poor kids who would not now be getting the drug. It was not put up as a cure but it did help prolong their life and I think, but don't quote me as I'm only a secretary not a medical expert, I think it also helped with the pain.'

'So how did it all play out?'

'Well, the drug never got funded. Apparently, the money was needed elsewhere.'

'Do you know where?' asked Hope, a little too strongly and the woman recoiled slightly.

'No, I'm only a secretary. But Judy, sorry, Mrs Finnieston, she started to drink more in the office. And she also started getting visits from a senior doctor.'

'Did you know him?' asked Ross gently.

'No, but then that was not unusual. His name was Dunnet or Daniels or something beginning with 'D'. He was never in the diary, always unannounced and she never failed to see him. I know there were frosty moments but other than that I don't know what they spoke of. As I said, I'm only a secretary—I only hear half a story.'

Ross saw the woman to a waiting taxi, taking her home number in case they needed further clarification. On returning, he found Hope still in the same seat, head in her hands.

'There's never enough, is there? I thought we were going to get it all on a plate but guess what? The main player is dead, and we don't even have a name for the other star of the story, just an initial.'

'But if Macleod's hunch is right about this being personal then we have something to go on. We need to find out who was affected by that drug not coming into use and we need to find out where the money that was withdrawn from it went. If we get that, I bet we get the story.'

'Time for our ferret,' said Hope.

Ross drove the pair back to the hotel while the evening was starting to come in. The hired room where the team had been working was dark with only one light on. Stewart sat behind her laptop, looking like she had become a statue. As Hope entered the room, the woman did not lift her head but merely stared at the screen.

'How are things going?' asked Ross.

'Slow. I could do with more detail. It seems the stopping of the drugs was only picked up by one paper, a local one at that. Due to medical privacy, I'm having a hard time seeing who was on that trial without flagging up to our superiors what I am doing. But I have contacted the reporter on the story.'

'Careful,' said Hope, 'we can't have the press opening up about what we're up to. There'll be hell to pay from above. I reckon Dalwhinnie will be asking questions if we're not gone from here in a few days.'

'I did think of that. While I was researching all this, a call came in from Patrick Smythe. The rocket launcher lead has gone cold, especially after the attack. No one is saying anything to anyone. But I believed he could still be of help, so I asked him to come and join us here. I also lined up the journalist for an interview, or at least a meeting. I thought if Paddy Smythe met her then we could deny all knowledge of what we are doing.'

'Smart girl,' said Hope, and then realised not even Macleod called Stewart a girl to her face. 'When's Smythe due?'

'He's driving up as we speak but he said it'll be two or three when he gets here so I set the meeting for six in the morning down by the loch at Corpach. You could probably watch from a car if you want.'

Hope looked offended. 'I think I should attend with Mr Smythe. See what this journalist says.'

'No, you shouldn't,' said Ross. 'Stewart is just going off-line a bit; misunderstood how far she should have gone with this investigation. You know the exact limits. You should stay in the car with me, sir. In fact, better we are far away.'

'Of course, you're right, Ross. Need to play the game in case this goes wrong. Well, you should get to bed as you have an early start, Stewart.'

'No, Sarge. With due respect, you need me to do the spade work tonight on the computer and see what else we can dig up. I'll be fine but a coffee wouldn't go amiss.'

'There's a kettle round here somewhere,' said Hope.

'Actually,' said Stewart, 'I wouldn't mind a proper one if you can find somewhere decent to get one.'

'Me, too,' Ross piped up, 'if you're going, boss.'

'I don't remember Macleod running this service. Just make sure you find me something.'

Hope exited the hotel and drove the car in Fort William looking for an open coffee shop. She eventually decided to grab some coffee from a supermarket café that was still open. It was at least properly made coffee and not some packet nonsense. As she carried the three coffees out in a cardboard holder, Hope felt her mobile go. She waited until she got to the car and placed the coffees on the roof, and saw the number was still ringing. It was Macleod.

'Seoras, I'm sorry. I should have called. How is she?'

'Long operation and she's still in a coma but they are expecting her to come out of it soon. How she'll be, they don't know. Nobody knows anything. How many years at medical school? And they know nothing.'

I didn't even pray, thought Hope. 'How are you?'

'Awful, but I didn't ring to seek any counselling. Tell me about the case. I know you didn't ring to ask about Jane because you had a rocket attack. Tell me Parry isn't still chasing terrorists.'

'What makes you so sure it wasn't?'

'The same as you. The location's awful for an attack. Poor roads and mountains to scale to get away. Unless you're a local and know your way about. He's a local.'

Hope related all she knew to Macleod and when she got to the part about using Smythe, she heard a grunt form Macleod. 'Is that your way of not approving, Seoras?'

'No, you're doing the right thing. You shouldn't have to use people like Smythe. If the high and mighty Mr Parry would open his eyes. Smythe will do you well, trust me. But it's not how policing should be. Don't go yourself.'

'Of course not,' said Hope. 'Stewart's accompanying him.'

'Good. You can tell me how it goes tomorrow.'

'Of course, Seoras. You know I'd be there with you if I could.'

'You, Mackintosh, Stewart, even Jona Nakamura called. I'm

going to invite Ross along just for protection.'

'It's how well we regard you, Seoras.'

'As a boss?'

'As one of us. Try and sleep tonight. I need to go. This is the first coffee run I've done for my team and it'll be bloody freezing when I get back.'

Chapter 21

I t was five in the morning when Hope's mobile sounded, and Stewart advised her that Paddy Smythe was outside the hotel. Meeting Stewart in the lobby, they walked outside where a man was standing in a brown jacket. His left arm was missing and the jacket arm was pinned to the body. His hair was scruffy and he wore trainers that had seen better days.

Stewart strode over to him and shook hands, introducing the Irishman once again to her boss. Hope thought he was judging her, sizing her up but then he simply nodded his head, saying he was glad to meet her again.

After Stewart brought Smythe up to speed with everything, he breathed in deeply and looked at Hope. 'So, you're undercutting the big wigs then. Sure you want to do that?'

'We have a killer on the loose, Mr Smythe.'

'It's just Paddy, McGrath. Don't get me wrong, I am more than happy to go past the management, and I did when I was back in the force but just be careful you want the flak that comes with it. If you end up in a position that will embarrass them, don't. Ends up badly, I have found out to my cost. By all means, take down the bad guy but be sure to spread the triumph around. By the way, Macleod know you're doing this?'

'He does and he grunted when I told him,' said Hope, smiling.

'The man has a real issue with me. Good guy but he needs to see that sometimes things get fixed only when you bend the rules. Anyway, it's a gorgeous morning so how about we get ourselves a reporter, Kirsten.'

Hope shot her eyes at Stewart. Not many people got to call her Kirsten but then she was impressed with Smythe. Hope thought the man had the ability to stare, to assess you without giving the feeling he was undressing you, like many men.

Part of Hope was itching to go along with them but Ross had reminded her again last night to stay well clear. She noted that the part of the car park where they had met Smythe this morning was an alcove without cameras. Maybe he was used to operating like that, keeping things dark. But not Hope, so she was glad he had covered the bases for her.

Stewart walked down to the town with Paddy, expecting there to be a stony silence but the truth was quite different.

'So, this guy is still on the loose. What makes you think he's tied into the whole hospital thing?'

'The boss said from the start the attacks did not feel like a terrorist but something different. No connections emerged from the first two whereas the last three have this NHS connection. We know that Finnieston was the target at the Waters of Nevis but the previous two we were unsure who the target was due to the shambles they were. Everything feels amateur, Paddy.'

'Certainly was when he picked up the gun, but he's not an idiot. But what about the first two attacks?'

'We believe they were practices,' said Stewart.

'Blimey, hell of a practice. You'd have to be seriously focused to do that to innocents if you have a target at the end. Whoever he is, someone must have hurt him bad. That's usually when the mist sets in and everything is justifiable.'

'We reckon he's local too because he disappears so easily. And as the boss says, who commits a terrorist attack on the Caledonian Canal. There's plenty of other more meaningful targets.'

'True, Kirsten. Now remember, you're just my niece. And lose the glasses, they give you away.' Stewart removed her lenses and struggled to see close in. The distant horizon was pretty clear but her hand was not.

'Don't ask me to read anything, Paddy, I'm blind at three inches right now.'

The sun was rising but the air was cool, and the grass had a spread of dew on it. The loch at Corpach already had a number of boats setting sail down the passage and the locks were in full swing. Stewart saw an older woman standing on the edge of the land looking out to the loch, her brown hair barely moving. It was short and thinned out but had been permed into a pleasing shape and no doubt held together by copious amounts of laquer like her grandmother had used. She was dressed in a smart overcoat and she wore tights and smart-but-practical black shoes.

'Caroline Urquhart,' said Paddy suddenly. 'I thought you'd given up this game. How the blazes are you?' The Ulsterman stepped forward throwing his arm around the woman and they embraced strongly.

'No one said it was you, Paddy. Still enjoying the cloak and dagger.'

'Just helping out some friends, passing on some messages. This is Kirsten by the way, an interested party, we'll say no more. Don't worry, Kirsten, Caroline is good at keeping a secret. An old school reporter.'

'No so old, Paddy. Well, actually too old for these early starts, even in summer.'

'Tell me about it. So, what's the deal with this NHS issue about the leukaemia drug funding? You had a story going on it?'

The woman pointed to a small bench and the three of them walked to it and sat down. The woman looked at Paddy and then raised her hand touching his chin. 'It's good to see you. I still remember that night. I wouldn't be feeling the sharpness of the morning if it weren't for you.'

'Well, you were too good to be taken out by getting too close to a story. But I thought you would be on a beach somewhere by now, making a toy boy work for his keep.'

Caroline laughed. 'I'd shrivel like a raisin in any heat. The Ulster body is not meant for that sort of heat.' And there it was. A slight twang, that harsh tone when she said the word Ulster. Paddy spoke in his dialect and accent all the time even if he refined it somewhat for his audience, but Caroline almost sounded Scottish until her roots were betrayed by the name of her home.

'I'd have been out by now except for this story I followed. I got a tipoff about a bit of commotion in the NHS—bullying, it was described as initially. It was occurring in, or at least had occurred, in Fort William Hospital. It's not a massive hospital but it has a number of departments. It involved a young courier and a senior consultant on the way up. I never got the consultant's name but I know the man at the receiving end was Peter Chen, although he never admitted it personally. My informant, Amanda Forsythe, was a nurse in the hospital and a friend of Peter but she left the country for New Zealand soon after.

'It was all rumours until I was contacted by a young girl in HR who snuck me out some emails from the senior HR manager for the area to Judy Finnieston. Now this baffled me, because Finnieston is finance and would have nothing to do with such a thing. But it discussed the arranging of a particular company to take receipt of funds for an office upgrade, in fact an entire building. Again, nothing unusual except the money was coming from the leukaemia drug funding that was about to happen.

'Again, this is all a bit shady but there was nothing to pin my hat on, until the HR girl told me she had seen the new building interior and there was no way it was worth the money paid for it. Now this was a story developing, so I managed to get in under false pretences and sure enough, the funding in no way matched the changes. Even dealing with the structure would not have covered it.

'Did you have any actual evidence of the cost and of the monies truly spent?' asked Paddy.

'None. My HR girl was trying to sneak me out some of it but then Peter Chen died, and she got spooked. I just thought it was a random terrorist attack that killed him on the ferry but now you are here, I guess that might not be the case.'

'It sounds like it wasn't,' said Stewart. 'Can you tell us the consultant's name?'

'Sorry, it never came out. And that's where I got to as well. When Chen died, I reckoned I should take a step back. I'm wary of getting too close, Paddy. You might not be here to pull me out this time. And like you said, I should really be retired.'

'You'll bury us all, Caroline. Did Chen have a partner?'

'If he did, it was kept quiet. But he sounds like a good starting place. If you can get at his personal effects and that, you might get a number or two.'

Paddy sat back, as if in thought and Stewart leaned across him. 'Caroline, did you have any contact with anyone who would have lost out from the drug funding not occurring?'

'There was a group who started up but they faded pretty quickly when they saw it was a done deal. None of them came my way and I couldn't get any of them to talk to me. There was talk of a legal challenge, but initial enquiries said there was no grounds for complaint as the money had never actually been allotted to the leukaemia drug, only talked about, and maybe a few false promises given. But nothing in black and white.'

'Thanks, Caroline,' said Paddy, 'now take the advice of an old friend and get some lotion and a towel and find a beach somewhere to lie back and enjoy the view.'

'You want to join me?' asked Caroline, a cheeky look on her face.

'Too late, a little woman from Stranraer sails my boat these days, literally, too.'

Caroline stood up and Paddy embraced her again. 'Good to see you. Walk away from this one, please; leave it up to us and we'll get you what we can when it's all over.'

On the walk back to the hotel, Stewart watched Smythe's face which seemed to be deep in thought. Her own mind was racing too, but whereas she was thinking about how best to connect the dots in the case, Smythe seemed to be reminiscing earlier times with Caroline.

On reaching the hotel, Smythe bade farewell before he was invited inside, and Stewart found her boss eagerly awaiting developments in the hired room. Before Hope and Ross, she detailed out the conversation and then watched her interim boss stand up and pace the room.

'Okay,' said Hope, 'given we have nothing concrete, let's get something. But we tread carefully. I'll check the next of kin for Peter Chen because as a victim we would have had to tell his next of kin. I can probably do that fairly quietly. You two get over to Martin Doonan. He has to be involved in this, so be hard on him and see what he knows. He's involved in our case so we can do that in near immunity from above. We also need to get a contact for the support group that was setting up to challenge the decision about the leukaemia drug. If we knew the people involved, then it might give us a possible attacker. At the moment someone attached to Chen would seem ideal, but we should cover the leukaemia drug line, too.'

'Once we speak to Doonan, I'll get some details on this leukaemia group and try and get some details from them,' said Stewart.

'Given the frequency with which this person has committed these attacks we need to expect another in the next few days. Maybe this consultant will be a target. So best speed, team.' Hope watched her colleagues leave the room and picked up the phone to call the co-ordinating desk for the terrorist team. Speaking to a low-level constable, she got an address for a Jason Holt, the next of kin for Peter Chen.

'I wouldn't bother trying to talk to him, though,' said the constable, 'he didn't want to know. Couldn't get us out of there quick enough. Not sure how bothered he really was. Maybe he was just sharing a flat.'

Or maybe he was scared witless about something being found out. Or maybe he was the killer? Although why kill Peter? No, Hope, that doesn't make sense.

With thoughts ringing around her head, Hope nearly didn't hear the call coming in on the landline. 'Yes,' she said, a little flustered, 'what is it?'

'Hello, ma'am, it's Sergeant Ferguson here, from Fort William station. I have just had a man walk in and say he knows your man from the photofit you issued to the public.'

'That's great,' said Hope. 'We're all on our way out at the moment and it's a rush so can you take details and any other information the man has and ring me with it. Don't let him go until you have passed the information to me.'

'Certainly, ma'am. I'll report directly to you as soon as I have it.'

Hope grabbed her jacket and slung it round her shoulders. After so few breaks, they were tumbling in fast. She needed the story to make sense of all of this and she had too few officers to be everywhere they needed to be. But the clock was ticking. Five incidents, a copious number of bodies. It was time to end this, whatever the agenda behind it was.

Chapter 22

J ason Holt lived in a small house that backed onto the Fort William shinty pitch. The sun was shining brightly as Hope approached the house and she saw a pale looking thin man in the garden, attending to some red flowers. Hope had no idea about flowers and simply spoke about them in colours. *Macleod would know what they were,* she thought, with Jane bringing him on side in the garden. Her heart sank for a moment at her boss's predicament but then she focused on the task in hand.

'Jason Holt?' The man looked up from his flowers.

'Who's asking?

'DS Hope Macleod, sir. I need to talk to you about your deceased friend, Peter Chen.'

The man stood up tall and Hope saw he was almost taller than her but was much thinner, like a stereotypical English gent. But the accent was Scottish. 'Friend, he was more than a friend. We lived here together for ten years.'

'My apologies, sir, I did not know. It must have hit you hard losing him on the ferry like that.'

The man bowed his head and when he raised it there were tears in his eyes. 'Of course, it did, and then to have one of your insensitive uniforms round here almost accusing me of doing it, simply because I was asleep at the time. No alibi, they said.'

'I don't think you did it, sir, but I think Peter had a history that caused it. Did he have some problems at work?'

Jason Holt stared at Hope, eyes still red and she could tell he was gauging her.

'I'm not here to upset the apple cart, Jason, but I have a murderer who has killed your lover and many more people besides. And I think Peter was the target on that day. I also know other NHS workers were the targets the other days. So, I want to know about his past, at the hospital. I need to understand who is coming after these people. And I think you can tell me. Maybe we can give him something in his time of rest.'

'Like what?' spat Jason. 'It was hard enough being gay in that place, but they took it all from him. Don't you understand there's nothing you can give him back, nothing you can give me. Oh, they tried to give us money, but Peter was too good for that. Gave it away to an AIDS charity. They stopped him from getting help, pressurised him into silence. And I lost him back then, not last week.'

'What happened?' asked Hope.

'And I tell you so you can do what? Stop somebody from killing those people. I heard who died at Nevis, Judy Finnieston. The bitch had dirt all over her hands. She should have stopped it, but she backed him, backed that filth.'

The man was starting to rant now, tears dripping from his eyes and Hope was struggling to keep up. The conversation was beginning to run away from her and she had to get it back before this became a public spectacle in the street.

'Mr Holt, I have to warn you that if you have information that could assist me in my enquiries and you willingly withhold that, then I will arrest you for obstruction. I don't want to burden you more than you have been, but you will leave me no choice.'

'Really, you'd nick me while those bastards run around. Well, let him kill them, whoever it is. Doing a job I wish I could do myself. Give him a knighthood—that's what I say.'

Hope could see the man was reeling with grief, but she needed to understand the situation. 'Mr Holt, he killed Peter, too. Why? I need to know why. Do you understand he's not your avenging angel? He killed your Peter. I need to bring him to justice for that. Tell me what trouble Peter had.'

'Trouble,' sniffed Jason. 'It was more than trouble. Repeatedly, it happened. He was meant to be leading Peter, showing him what to do. It was Peter's big moment working with a man he idolised. But he came on to Peter, then cornered him. Peter was so timid, would never hurt anyone or defend himself. The gentlest soul. I could tell at night that bastard had been at him again.'

'Are you saying someone abused Peter, sexually?'

Jason Holt dropped to his knees, his head in his hands and began to weep uncontrollably. Hope jumped the hedge and knelt down beside the man. 'I'm so sorry, sir, maybe we should take this inside.' Helping the man up, they stumbled together towards the door of the house. Hope felt her mobile vibrating in her pocket, but she knew she could not leave the man in this situation. Entering the house, she walked with him to a sunroom at the back which looked onto the shinty pitch. There she deposited Jason Holt in a chair.

'Mr Albert Dunbar is who you want, officer. He's a tall strong man with wide shoulders and he liked how much smaller Peter was than him. I have had to endure over the last two years, nights of Peter telling me about it, sitting up in bed as he cried on my shoulder, and all the while, Peter incapable of being intimate again. So yes, you see why I say let him kill them all. May it be with as much pain as they can be dealt.'

Hope felt ashamed being in this man's grief, but she had to find out the truth. 'So, they paid Peter off?'

'He complained and it went up to his boss, Martin Doonan, complete shit of a man. He panicked and it went to Judy Finnieston who decided to hush it all up. Mr Dunbar was pioneering flagship methods in his field and they could not have him sullied. He was bringing in big companies to invest. And they paid Peter off.'

'But how? It's the NHS; they don't have that much money.' Hope couldn't see the last link, but she knew it was there.

'Like I know or care.' Jason collapsed into tears again and Hope politely excused herself retreating to the hall to pick up her missed call.

'Ma'am, I interviewed the gentleman as asked and he says the man is Fergus Fletcher, a one-time associate of his although he has not seen him in nearly two years. Fergus used to attend a protest group the gentleman ran and it all ended a bit badly and the man never saw Fergus again. He says the drawing is remarkably close to the likeness, but he may be able to get you a photograph.'

'Keep him there, Sergeant; whatever happens, don't let him leave. I think he could be giving us our terrorist.' As soon as the word had left her mouth Hope knew she should not have said it. They were meant to be under the radar, but this would get word spreading. It would go very simply by someone asking the Sergeant who that was and then they would get excited about catching the long-wanted terrorist and word would filter upstairs and then they would ask what was going on.

'Very good, ma'am, I'll await your arrival.' And the telephone went down. Hope cursed herself for being so stupid. She dialled Ross' number and he answered immediately.

'What have you got from Doonan?'

'Nothing,' said Ross, 'clammed up as soon as we started asking questions and wants a lawyer before he speaks. Sorry, boss, but his wife is too wise, saw us coming a mile off. But he knows something.'

'Darn right he does,' said Hope. 'Peter Chen was sexually abused while working for him and Doonan assisted in the cover up. That's why he doesn't want to speak. It was committed by Mr Albert Dunbar. Get onto that and don't worry about Doonan; let him sit in an interview room. Get Stewart to find Dunbar's movements for the next few days. I think he'll be the target.'

'Sure, boss but I'm not following. What did Judy Finnieston have to do with it then?'

'She organised the cover up. Whoever the killer is, he's going round them. I think Dunbar is next. I'm going to the station in town to see a man who thinks he can identify the killer from our photofit. And by the way, it's going upstairs. I blurted out the man in the photofit was our terrorist and the Sergeant at the station has someone who can identify him.'

'That'll go like wildfire.'

'Damn right, Ross, so keep out of the light and bounce any calls you get.'

'I hear you, boss; will be in touch.'

Hope's heart was pumping. How had she made such a mess

of this? But there was nothing for it but to see it through. Popping her head back into the sunroom, Hope thanked Jason Holt for his time and left the man sobbing. There was no time to feel bad about this, she told herself, but she did anyway. Once in the car, she made directly for the station.

The desk Sergeant was beaming when Hope entered the station and happily pointed her to the interview room where her witness awaited. In the rather barren room, sitting behind a simple table and holding a cup of coffee in a plastic cup, sat a small man with narrow round glasses.

'Hello, Sergeant. The desk officer said you were a Sergeant, detective though I bet. Arthur Brownlea, a Yorkshire man abroad shall we say. Ten years up here in the land of Braveheart. Almost a local you could say.'

Like heck you could say, thought Hope, but she had no time for the man's pomposity. 'Mr Brownlea, I need to impress on you that we do not have a lot of time here and so I want you to be succinct in your response and try and help me out. The desk Sergeant said you thought you could identify the man in the photofit picture. Is that correct?'

'Why yes, ma'am, like he was my own son. It's Calum Gordon. He used to be a member of our action group against the NHS, or rather certain elements within the NHS because as we all know it is a fine institution and the envy of many countries because—'

'Mr Brownlea, I don't need commercials, just details. What was your group against?'

'Actually, we were for, not against. We wanted a new drug that was in the pipeline to be offered to leukaemia suffers, particularly children. We fought for the funding and it was there, a promise made verbally to us. My own niece still suffers from it.'

'What happened to the funding if it was promised?'

'We never knew. I think it went elsewhere but they would never say. Their finance bod, Finnieston, explained it all away but no one really understood. But Calum took it bad. His wife died in childbirth giving birth to Alison his daughter. And then she got leukaemia and he saw the drug as a saviour. Who knows if it would have been, but she went downhill and died shortly after the drug was cancelled, or never acquired as they put it. Calum had a go at me but really he was just angry at them. I understood, never blamed him. He would take himself off out into the countryside in those camouflage trousers of his and simply become more and more bitter. Then he stopped coming to our meetings. Never seen him since.'

'Would you say he had a hatred of those who denied the drug?'

'Very much, ma'am. I swear he could have ripped them apart. But he was the silent type. Slow to act but devastating when he did. He bottled it all up, never said anything, even at our support groups. Was all his to carry.'

A knock came at the door and it was opened by the desk sergeant. 'Apologies, ma'am, but I have a Mr Parry on the line; says he wants to speak to you now. Said not to take no for answer. Sorry.'

'Oh, hell,' thought Hope but she rose serenely and apologised to Brownlea for the interruption. Walking to the desk to take the call from Parry, Hope looked at the desk Sergeant who pursed his lips and made a shaking motion with his head. It did not look like a friendly call.

'McGrath, what are you doing? DCI Dalwhinnie was to make it clear to you that you were simply to close up the copycat case and then go home. Instead I hear you have the identity of our terrorist. All this while I am looking right at him. We are about to collect him, so if you don't mind, just sit tight and your DCI will have a word with you.'

'But it's not him, sir. The killer is no terrorist; he's an aggrieved father whose daughter had leukaemia and died.'

'I don't want to know about it, Sergeant. There's no need to try and impress just because you got to step into the limelight. Macleod was wrong—they should have sent someone in at his grade. After what Allison had said … '

Hope stopped listening. It would be all right. Dalwhinnie would come and she could explain. As long as nothing else happened.

' … and don't leave the station, McGrath. If you do, I'll consider it insubordination and get you busted right back to uniform. Now if I can kindly get back to my terrorist.'

Hope calmly placed the telephone on the receiver. The desk Sergeant looked at her awkwardly. 'I think he's having a bad day,' said Hope and smiled. Her mobile then rang.

'Boss, it's Stewart. I found Mr Dunbar on the web. Apparently, he's addressing some pharmaceutical companies today at Fort Augustus. He'll be on a boat making a speech. It's listed on one of the NHS diary pages. It's in an hour's time.'

Hope froze as Stewart spoke. It dawned on her what Macleod had said about the first attack being amateurish. Calum Gordon was prepping himself by having a trial run. He knew this date was coming.

'Stewart, we need to get to Fort Augustus, fast.'

'The road's blocked. We've already left but we heard there's a load of logs deposited across the road at Aberchalder. You have to take the long way round at Invergarry to Invermoriston.

Ross is going as quick as he can.'

'I'll be there!' Hope hung up and looked at the desk sergeant who had heard the whole call. 'If DCI Dalwhinnie comes, tell her I was called away urgently.'

'Shall I say where to, ma'am?'

'No, sergeant. She can call me.'

With the road blockage, time was going to be against them. She wanted to call for backup coming in from the north, down from Inverness but any deployment was bound to be spotted, especially as she had Dalwhinnie now on her back. Surely there was someone she could call. Hope pressed the phone book on her mobile and at the top above all other numbers sat an image of her boss. She could not. She should not ask him. Then her thumb pressed down on Macleod's face.

Chapter 23

Macleod looked at the woman lying on the bed, her head wrapped up where the surgery had taken place. At home, she had always been so full of life and it was her total lack of movement that was grabbing him inside. His gut felt sick and the only comfort was the rhythmic rise and fall of her chest showing she was still breathing. Jane had picked up his life at a time when he thought that side of life was long gone.

In his hand he clutched the mobile phone. He could hear Hope questioning if he was still there. She was asking for help, help to stop a killer. Inside he was torn between being there for Jane and the call to the hunt, something that was in him, always ready to be awakened. He kidded himself he was trying to decide, but he knew the instinct deep inside was rising. There would never be something that could pull him from his duty, his calling.

'Don't go,' he whispered to her through the window, 'at least not until I'm back.' Macleod turned away from the window and strode towards the door at the end of the hospital corridor. 'I'll be there, McGrath. Get there as soon as you can.' And he closed the call.

The car park at Raigmore hospital was full but Macleod let

the traffic pass away before him, breathing deeply inside. He had been emotionally battered, had seen his beloved cling to life. But now he had to focus, and he did not do that by getting angry. The shoppers and workers in Inverness packed the road but Macleod waited until he crossed the bridge over the River Ness and then had passed the Botanic gardens before he opened up the throttle on the car. In his head, images of Fort Augustus rolled past, mainly of days out. He could not remember having to deal with any trouble there, let alone an assassination attempt.

The bright side of being a man who was technically off duty and watching his partner fight for her life was that no one would call him. They would never suspect Hope would bring her stricken boss into this mess. But then they did not know the affection in which he held her. Yes, affection was the right word. He was deeply fond of her although he had to keep a distance as her boss. But she was dedicated and kind. Most of all, she was like him deep down. That hunter's instinct and determination not to give up. Well, he was not having his star sergeant falling a cropper to the incompetence of those above.

The back end of the car swung out at a corner and Macleod only just recovered it. In truth, he did not like driving but that was no excuse for sloppiness. His anger nearly got the better of him there. When the dust settled there would be enough time for anger and recriminations, but not now. There was a life to save.

As the waters of Loch Ness passed by on his left-hand side, it was not long before he found himself at the turn at Invermoriston. If Hope were coming up from the south, she would come this way too, due to the diversion. He called her but she said she was behind him; Ross and Stewart were probably nearer but Macleod would be first.

'In that case, Hope, I'll go for the boat he's making the speech or talk on; that way I can get him inside. You go for the shooter, same with Ross and Stewart.'

'Okay, Seoras, good plan, and how is—'

'Don't ask. Just don't. I have work to do.'

Fort Augustus was located at the southern end of Loch Ness and had a set of locks which boats utilised to climb up to the narrower water which continued the Caledonian Canal. There was a main road that ran through the small village and crossed a bridge over the canal at the bottom of the lock steps. There was a similarity to Neptune's Steps at Fort William, something that was not escaping Macleod's thoughts. *It'll be a gun attack. It was a practice; maybe the bomb was too. Except the bomb was too large; he didn't like it—wanted to target more precisely.*

Hope had briefly stated something about Calum Gordon, the attacker, but Macleod could not take in all that detail. Instead he was concentrating on his own task, to find and secure Dunbar and then everyone else out of the line of fire. In doing so he would be in that line of fire. He tried not to think about that.

Macleod crossed the first stone bridge in his car and noticed the sheer number of tourists about in the bright sunshine. His car had the air conditioning on, and he felt cool, almost cold, but everyone outside was in shorts and t-shirts. There were families, old people on a day out, dogs being walked, and ice creams being eaten. It was a fine day at the lochside, and everyone was blissfully unaware of the carnage about to happen.

Macleod approached the swing bridge over the canal and simply parked up on the road that ran on the nearside of the canal. Someone shouted about his parking, but he ignored them, scanning the area.

In front of him was the swing bridge crossing the entrance to the lock steps. On his right, he saw them climb up to a flatter part near the top where he knew there were berths at the side of the canal. On his left the water was low and ran out to the loch. There were berths there too, so the actual boat could be anywhere. He looked for any signs of an advertisement but there were none. The event was small scale, non-public, so that was to be expected.

At the first attack he shot up the steps, thought Macleod, and turned right and began to run up the side of the lock steps. There was a road on either side and a number of shops, eateries and visitor centres which were overflowing, and Macleod found himself bumping into various day trippers as he made his way up the hill. A pair of camouflage trousers caught his eye but then he saw the woman who was wearing them, and he disregarded her. There were too many people.

As he continued up the canal side, he saw a large motor cruiser at the top. It was berthed on the far side of the canal at the top of the steps and its top deck was open and exposed. Although not exceptionally large, Macleod could see a screen and a number of people in suits and dresses milling about on board; their garb was too much for the day's heat and he recognised a formal function and ran hard towards it.

The lock operation was in full swing and as he neared the top lock, he realised it was about to open. Macleod ran towards it, spying the top of the lock gates which had retaining bars on either side so they could be crossed when the gate was closed. But now it was opening there would be a gap between the gates. Macleod ran on regardless.

'Stop!' yelled a gatekeeper, 'don't be an idiot.' Macleod saw the man coming towards him as Macleod was just short of the gate.

'Police! Move aside,' yelled Macleod but the man continued to block Macleod's path. Dropping his shoulder, he hit the man about rib height and sent him spinning. Recovering from that knock, Macleod ran across the top of the gate and saw it opening as he was on top of it. The gates were parting, opening away from each other and the line of the lines was becoming closer to the perpendicular than the acute angle they previously were. He grabbed the rail at the end of the gate, swung hard on it and let go, jumping with all he had. One foot found an edge, his hand grabbed a rail and he swung out on top of the gate. Like a football match, there were cries from the onlookers and he felt the muscles in his arms and back strain. But he managed to retain his balance and haul himself forward, running across this new gate to the canal edge.

'Are you mad, man?' yelled a lockkeeper at him but Macleod turned up hill and ran for the large cruiser berthed at the edge. There was a gang plank leading onto the boat with a tall, heavily built man at the entrance in a dark suit. Everything about him said bouncer and Macleod thought it best to get his words in early for the man was starting to come to a threatening pose at the advancing Macleod.

'Police! Is Dunbar aboard, Albert Dunbar?'

'Can I see some ID, sir?' asked the man, now stepping across Macleod and fully blocking his way.

Macleod reached inside his jacket and hauled his warrant card in front of the man. 'DI Macleod. Shift it, sunshine!'

'Do you have a warrant?'

I don't have time for this thought Macleod and brought an

201

explosive knee up to the man's groin, making him double over. Ignoring him, Macleod ran onto the cruiser and entered the lower deck. There was a passageway and he saw a number of doors into cabins, but he needed to go up. At the end of the passageway was a round set of stairs and he ran for them. Gold and silver were the order of the day in the passage, but Macleod ignored the ostentatiousness and climbed up the stairway, gasping for breath. Once on the upper deck, he saw a man coming towards him dressed in white jacket and with a peaked cap. On his shoulders were epaulettes and his face looked angry.

'What are you doing here? Get off my vessel!'

'Albert Dunbar? Where is Albert Dunbar? Police! I'm the police.'

'Mr Dunbar's just started his lecture at the rear of the vessel. You'll have to wait, sir. I need to see some credentials and—'

'He's in the open? Move, man.'

'Don't tell me what—'

But Macleod was already at the man and shoving him sideways. Looking beyond, he saw a white screen and a man beside it, pointing at something on the screen. Beyond him sat a small audience who were beginning to look at Macleod charging down the deck.

'Albert Dunbar? Are you Albert Dunbar?'

'Why yes, what is it? How dare you interrupt.'

'Police! Come with me, now.'

The man placed both hands on his hips. He was at least six feet four and Macleod could see tackling him and hauling him away was going to be tough but that was not his main concern. Scanning over the edge of the deck, Macleod saw people milling about, except for one. From the high deck,

Macleod could see about halfway down the lock gates and on the edge of the canal a man was standing and dropping down a bag. It was long and thin, and he was unzipping something.

'Get down,' shouted Macleod, 'there's a gun.'

'A what? Don't be ridiculous. We're in Fort Augustus. I'm giving a lecture.'

Macleod saw the weapon being raised and also saw the man in the white uniform coming down the deck after him followed by the bouncer he had disabled on the side of the canal. There was no time to debate anything. Macleod ran forward driving at Dunbar's legs hitting the knees from slightly behind so as to make him crumple. As Macleod hit the deck, he heard a rasp of gunfire ripping across the boat.

* * *

Ross could hear the gunfire as he pulled into Fort Augustus, crossing the stone bridge. He flicked on the blue lights and sirens as Stewart peered out of the window trying to spot the shooter. Cars and people were fleeing the scene as he negotiated the swing bridge, nearly knocking down a mother carrying a small child.

'Can you see him, Stewart?'

'Far side up the steps, over halfway up.' They heard more gunfire and Ross clocked the shooter. Standing in camouflage trousers and wearing a hooded top, he was liberally spraying bullets at a cruiser that was further up the locks. Ross pushed the accelerator and spun the car onto the road that ran parallel with the steps on the far side of the bridge.

'What are you doing? He's got a rifle and he's firing bullets like crazy!' shouted Stewart.

'Someone's got to stop him,' said Ross, 'or he'll take out how many people. Keep low!' Stewart's eyes went wide as she watched Ross drive at speed up the small parallel road before breaking through the wooden fence and driving directly at the shooter. But he saw them coming and stepped out onto the lock gate which was closed. He fired at the car and Ross lost control. The car drove on into one of the retainers on top of the lock gate and then spun precariously onto the edge.

'Out!' shouted Stewart and clicked her belt's fastening, before opening the door. As she tumbled and then scrambled backwards, she heard the car being shot up. Looking over her shoulder she could not see Ross and then watched in horror as the car tumbled into the lock between the gates.

'Ross!' she screamed. In her head she saw a woman laughing and the trauma of their last case came back to her. She had chased a suspect who then killed a man in front of her, a man who had effectively saved Stewart's life. Her body froze and her mind raced.

Everywhere was chaos. People ran this way and that while the man stood on the lock gates continuing to fire at the vessel. Stewart scrambled backwards on her bottom trying to get over to the road and lie flat so the shooter would not be able to sight her. Her body was shaking, and a cold sweat was on her face. All she could say was, 'Ross, Ross, where are you?'

* * *

Hope had to abandon the car just short of Fort Augustus and ran across the stone bridge opposite to the general flow of escaping holidaymakers. As she reached the swing bridge, Hope saw the shooter further up the lock gates, standing on one of the gates firing at the vessel above him. Hope ran in behind one of the buildings on her side of the lock gates and began to make her way along the rear of the houses and shops, hurdling walls and hedges. If she could get close enough, she might be able to surprise him. After hurdling over what seemed like endless obstructions, she heard the gunfire stop and rounded the corner of a building to see what the shooter was up to.

Calum Gordon was walking off the lock gate onto the far side and Hope saw her opportunity. Without a word or a cry to halt, she ran hard up the green slope to the lock gate and began to run across it. The man looked round, realised Hope was after him and then started sprinting towards a bag on the ground. But Hope saw someone running towards the bag as well. The woman was small and dressed in black with a pair of glasses on her face.

As Hope cleared the lock gates, she saw Stewart reaching down for the bag, but Calum Gordon swung his gun at her and struck her on the face sending her spinning backwards towards the ground. As Hope closed on Gordon, he was reaching into the bag and she flung herself onto his back.

Hope was almost six feet tall and the man was significantly smaller but he managed to take the weight of her jumping on him and then spun over to drop her onto her back with him and his gun coming down on her, his back to her front. As she lay winded, he climbed to his feet and grabbed a cartridge from the bag, slamming it into the rifle. As Hope fought to get back to her feet, she saw the barrel of the rifle pointing at her and recoiled in panic. There was nowhere to go, nowhere to run; he was only a few feet away and she was prone on the ground.

As she looked at the man's face, she saw no emotion, no anger, just dead eyes. He was perhaps more chilling than any psychopath she had ever seen, and he was tucking the rifle tight into his shoulder, ready to fire. But behind Gordon, she saw a figure, soaked and in a suit. It was running at full tilt towards Gordon and the gunman clocked the look in Hope's eyes, turning round to see what was approaching. The figure jumped the gunman and a shot rang out.

Hope saw Ross on top of the man and scrambled over to jump on Gordon. Ross took a punch to the head but Hope drove a fist to Gordon's face and then watched the gun slip from his grasp. She grabbed it with one hand and threw it as best as she could away from them. Gordon reached for her, snaking an arm around her throat.

But Ross was back on his feet and fell on the man, driving an elbow to his head. Hope was released and she reached for her handcuffs. Together Ross and Hope managed to roll the man over and pull his arms up behind his back. The cuffs clicked on him and they held the man on the ground.

Stewart struggled to her feet, her face bleeding badly and her glasses gone. She was shaking, and her forehead was dripping sweat onto the blood from her cheek. Across from the scene, a man was standing with a mobile phone, the device trained on the small cohort of police officers and their captured shooter.

'Tell me, just tell me you have dialled 999,' Hope shouted at the man. Standing in his shorts and T-shirt, the man simply smiled. 'No, really, have you dialled for the police? Ambulance, too.'

The man smiled again and then turned to shout over to a woman half hiding behind a building on the far side of the road.

'I think that's Italian,' said Ross. 'Do you think he got his target?'

'No,' said Hope. Look up there.' She pointed to the cruiser the man had been firing at. Standing at the edge of the upper deck in a long coat was Macleod. There was no smile, no wave or celebratory fist in the air. Instead a simple nod came from him to his team below. Hope raised her arm in response.

Chapter 24

Stewart sat in the rear of an ambulance with a paramedic attending to her battered face. Ross was standing outside, awaiting an update on her injuries. Wrapped in a foil blanket, he seemed to be extremely cheery to Hope who was handing over what she knew to DCI Dalwhinnie. The woman was looking sombre, but Hope was simply exhausted.

Two of the invited guests on the cruiser had been shot but were expected to pull through their injuries with no permanent damage. A lucky break. Of the general public surrounding the incident, one man had been injured falling into one of the locks as he tried to run away from the shooting, a car had crashed into another causing whiplash injuries, and a child had suffered a broken leg in the crush to get away. All in all, a good result, Hope thought.

Hope had barely seen Macleod as he was dealing with the confusion on the cruiser and getting medical help to the injured parties. Calum Gordon was en route to Inverness station where he would be interviewed by DCI Dalwhinnie's team. Although she was feeling physically tired, Hope was also feeling vindicated, almost elated to be proved right, even more so for Macleod.

As Dalwhinnie was talking to Hope, Macleod made his way

down the side of the lock gates towards the ambulance that housed Stewart. There was no way he could have known she was inside, but he must have guessed given how Ross was hanging around outside. Hope watched him disappear inside for a minute before coming outside and shaking hands with Ross. Macleod's face was deadpan, but she heard him tell Ross he was glad Ross was okay and that he should be commended for the help he had given Hope.

And then he walked up to Hope as Dalwhinnie was talking to her, completely blanked the DCI and took Hope's hand. For a moment he locked eyes with her, then he shook her hand.

'Job done, Sergeant.'

'Just followed your line of thinking, sir.'

'No, you deserve the plaudits on this one. Always glad to help the team. Don't let them take the credit away from you. They screwed up.' And with that he walked off. There was blood on his shirt and he looked warm in his long coat, but the man was impassive.

'Macleod, I need to talk to you,' said Dalwhinnie. Macleod never even looked back but kept on walking. 'Detective Inspector, I need to talk to you. As your senior officer, I order you to come back.'

'His partner is possibly dying, ma'am,' said Hope, 'so with all due respect, I think he wants you to simply piss off.'

'Don't you be so insubordinate, sergeant, or I'll break your arse back to the beat.'

'If I had listened to that threat, you would have a lot of bodies to bury here and not simply wounded people. If you will excuse me for a moment, I think my team needs some attention.' Hope pulled her leather jacket up her shoulders and walked to the ambulance.

209

'They want to take Stewart up to Raigmore. I think she should go but she's wanting to stay and help,' said Ross.

'She should go. Dalwhinnie can take care of things; after all, we closed our copycat case,' smirked Hope. 'She can drop in and see the boss when she's done. I was going up that way anyway when we're complete.'

'I can't believe he came,' said Ross.

'Of course, you can. We're his team and he was the only one available. I just hope he didn't miss anything.'

* * *

Macleod sat in the sterile room and watched Jane breathing. Up and down, like she had done for the last few days, however many it was. He had no idea—the only intermission being his excursion to Fort Augustus. That was maybe two days ago and only a trip home to shower had kept him from her bedside. He knew it was pointless keeping this watch; after all, she could not hear him. If she woke, they would tell him. If she died, there would be a sombre and polite call. But this was the custom, useless as it was.

He had tried to pray and ended up talking to God more than offering up requests and thanks. But there was no answer to the questions of why, and when she would be coming round. In fact, the conversation felt very one-sided. But unlike sitting around waiting, it had not felt useless.

The sound of the door to the room opening made him look up and he saw Hope there with a bunch of flowers. She smiled awkwardly, looked at Jane, and then asked, 'No change?'

Macleod shook his head. 'So, they finally let you go?'

'Yes. They decided they couldn't do the interviews on their

210

own. Parry was noticeable by his absence and Dalwhinnie had so much humble pie in her mouth, it was almost hard to watch. But she never said she had got it wrong.'

Macleod looked out of the window at another day of glorious sunshine. 'It doesn't matter. And one day you'll get it wrong.'

'What about you?'

'I have got it wrong so often it hurts, but then you learn when you are right. This time everything screamed at me, every fibre of me said it wasn't a terrorist. Too amateur, too strange, none of it about the place or symbolism.'

'Calum Gordon was simply cut up about his child dying from leukaemia,' said Hope. 'When I interviewed him at Dalwhinnie's request, he confessed to it all. It took over a year in planning. He researched how to get a gun on the black market, where to find the explosives but that didn't go right. He got the amounts wrong. He practised archery out in the wilds away from everyone, had it all hidden away. But his greatest trick was finding Finnieston and actually romancing her and then becoming her lover. That's when he found out everything that had gone on. And he blamed them all.'

'But why different weapons?' asked Macleod.

'To make it seem like a terrorist attack, to make them think it was someone different. And he needed a practice, that was why he committed the first two attacks. The first was his way of practising for the attack on Dunbar at Fort Augustus. A similar set of locks and he knew the man would be on a boat. Well the *Lord of the Glens* was one vessel he could get a timetable for and which was reasonably high.'

'And Skye? Was that preparation for killing Judy Finnieston?'

'He reckoned a small bomb would do it but was shocked by the damage caused. It was strange; he didn't want others to suffer and yet he also believed a certain amount of collateral damage was warranted. Even during the Skye Bridge bombing, I couldn't get his rationale.'

Macleod stood and walked to the window, shaking his head. 'You won't get it. It's not rational, just what they convince themselves of. And the Skye Bridge—he was dressed as a woman.'

'Yes, convincingly, too.'

Macleod turned and smiled at Hope. 'Not to me. Something didn't sit or jiggle right. I have an eye for women, in case you had not spotted, Hope. I guess this was the one time it didn't get me into trouble. I had a good eye when I spotted Jane.'

Hope stood now and walked to the window throwing her arms around him from behind. She pulled him close in a hug and felt him relaxing into it, not from enjoyment but from need.

'And he decided on the rocket then for Finnieston. Cleaner I guess, and he had experience purchasing such items. I guess it all worked for him except the archery. Must be harder than it looks.'

Macleod fell silent and Hope continued to hug him by the window. Although he was speaking to her, Hope knew there was a part of him not there, a part of him that was taken by a fear of losing Jane.

'I prayed, you know. Last night, and the night before. In the hotel room. I have told Ross about it, what you had said about praying and he told me I should give it a go for you. It's funny though because I didn't really know what to say. Other than make Jane better.'

'Did he answer?'

'Doesn't he always? I thought you believed in prayer being

answered, that it was just you having difficulty with it.'

Macleod broke her hug and turned to face her. 'I have bloody well shouted and begged Him. I have bargained away the life of others, mine included, in an attempt to bring her back to me. And what has he said? Nothing! Not one word, not a passing comment from a friend or a hopeful moment for the doctors or nurses. There's been people from the church here praying and so damn optimistic about God bringing her through.

'And yet look at her, Hope. She was smashed by that bus. If she comes through, who knows how she'll be. They reckon she'll struggle to walk, struggle to regain any life like she had. Am I just bloody selfish wanting her back? If she comes back, will He heal her as well, because if not, I'm wondering if He's just more than a little bit cruel. But God knows, I want her back.'

'Seoras Macleod, you romantic fool!'

The pair turned to the speaker of these fresh words and saw Jane still lying there, her breathing her only movement. But then the lips moved although the eyes did not open.

'Don't I get a kiss? Get that fancy woman out of the way and get over here.'

Macleod brushed past Hope and bending down he wrapped his arms around Jane and kissed her on the lips. When he broke off, he raised himself and looked her up and down.

'How do you feel?'

'I don't, Seoras, I can't feel my legs or my arms. I did feel your kiss. But I can't feel my legs.' Jane started to sob. 'Dear God, is this it, Seoras? Help me.'

'I'll get the doctor,' said Hope, leaving the room.

Macleod sat on the bed and simply hugged his woman. *Is this what we get? Is this the best from you? Wasn't getting hit by a*

213

bus enough? She's the best thing you have given me and then you simply take her away? You hurt her? To hell with your providence.

That night Hope brought Macleod a coffee as Jane had fallen asleep. The doctors offered no idea on whether her legs would come back to her, or her arms. When Jane was sleeping, Macleod had popped to another ward to see Stewart who was having some work done to her face. The battering from the rifle had delivered more damage than at first thought. Her brother, who had enough social and physical difficulties of his own, had been in the room and Macleod saw someone else who had to care although injured. But now outside the hospital and sitting on a bench, Macleod drank the coffee Hope had bought him.

'This will take time and I may need a while off or at least part-time. I'll tell Dalwhinnie I don't want anyone else in but that you can run the team with me sitting over the top available at all times.'

'You take what you need, Seoras. I'll help where I can.'

'It's okay. Mackintosh rang and offered to help. She's still with us anyway and she feels a debt. I'm no use with the patient thing. Yes, I'd wipe Jane's bottom and lift her and all that, but she would know I'm not right with it. Having someone who can care properly will be good. It'll also keep Mackintosh busy. She's not come to terms with the way the surgery changed her.'

'That's understandable, sir.'

'Understanding's not the problem with her; it's getting her to believe she's still beautiful. You women think us men only see the outside. You've no idea how wrong you are. But go home, Hope. You've been under the cosh with the case. You and Jona. Go and have a girlie night watching chick flicks or whatever women do these days.'

'Not my style, sir, but we will chill out.'

Macleod watched Hope depart still drinking her coffee and then waved to her as her car drove past him when she exited the hospital grounds. His own coffee was now empty, and he placed it in a rubbish bin near the door of the hospital. He looked up to the fifth floor, where Jane was sleeping. *You better show me how to do this. I don't want providence. I want help. Just help me, because if you don't.* Macleod felt his hand clasp and his fist shake ever so slightly. With his rebuke at God complete, he walked through the sliding doors and into the next chapter of his life.

Read on to discover the Patrick Smythe series!

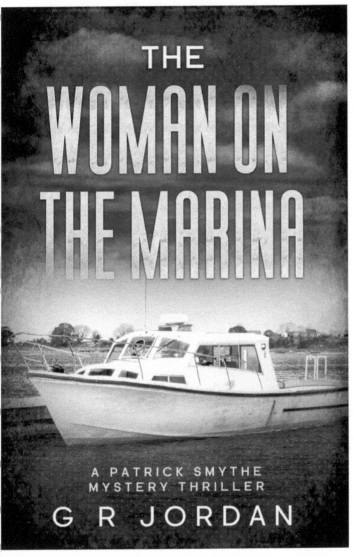

THE

WOMAN ON THE MARINA

A PATRICK SMYTHE MYSTERY THRILLER

G R JORDAN

Start your Patrick Smythe journey here!

Patrick Smythe is a former Northern Irish policeman who

after suffering an amputation after a bomb blast, takes to the sea between the west coast of Scotland and his homeland to ply his trade as a private investigator. Join Paddy as he tries to work to his own ethics while knowing how to bend the rules he once enforced. Working from his beloved motorboat 'Craigantlet', Paddy decides to rescue a drug mule in this short story from the pen of G R Jordan.

Join G R Jordan's monthly newsletter about forthcoming releases and special writings for his tribe of avid readers and then receive your free Patrick Smythe short story.

Go to https://bit.ly/PatrickSmythe for your Patrick Smythe journey to start!

About the Author

GR Jordan is a self-published author who finally decided at forty that in order to have an enjoyable lifestyle, his creative beast within would have to be unleashed. His books mirror that conflict in life where acts of decency contend with self-promotion, goodness stares in horror at evil, and kindness blindsides us when we at our worst. Corrupting our world with his parade of wondrous and horrific characters, he highlights everyday tensions with fresh eyes whilst taking his methodical, intelligent mainstays on a roller-coaster ride of dilemmas, all the while suffering the banter of their provocative sidekicks.

A graduate of Loughborough University where he masqueraded as a chemical engineer but ultimately played American football, Gary had worked at changing the shape of cereal flakes and pulled a pallet truck for a living. Watching vegetables freeze at -40'C was another career highlight and he was also one of the Scottish Highlands "blind" air traffic controllers.

These days he has graduated to answering a telephone to people in trouble before telephoning other people to sort it out.

Having flirted with most places in the UK, he is now based in the Isle of Lewis in Scotland where his free time is spent between raising a young family with his wife, writing, figuring out how to work a loom and caring for a small flock of chickens Luckily, his writing is influenced by his varied work and life experience as the chickens have not been the poetical inspiration he had hoped for!

You can connect with me on:

🌐 https://grjordan.com

📘 https://facebook.com/carpetlessleprechaun

Subscribe to my newsletter:

✉ https://bit.ly/PatrickSmythe

Also by G R Jordan

G R Jordan writes across multiple genres including crime, dark and action adventure fantasy, feel good fantasy, mystery thriller and horror fantasy. Below is a selection of his work. Whilst all books are available across online stores, signed copies are available at his personal shop.

A Just Punishment (Highlands & Islands Detective Book 8)
https://grjordan.com/product/a-just-punishment
A former convict, hung, drawn and quartered. Macleod called by name for his former actions. Can the Lewis detective find the righter of wrongs before the killer executes those close to Macleod?

As his partner recovers from a devastating accident, Macleod faces a hidden face from his past who is determined to see justice truly done. But as the killer punishes each justifiable victim, Macleod feels the target of the attacks is moving coming closer to home. In a devastating finale, Macleod must rely on his younger Sergeant, Hope McGrath, more than he has ever before.

The pain you deal will be visited upon you tenfold!

Highlands and Islands Detective Thriller Series

https://grjordan.com/product/waters-edge

Join stalwart DI Macleod and his burgeoning new female DC McGrath as they look into the darker side of the stunningly scenic and wilder parts of the north of Scotland. From the Black Isle to Lewis, Mull to Harris and across to the small Isles, the Uists and Barra, this mismatched pairing follow murders, thieves and vengeful victims in an effort to restore tranquillity to the remoter parts of the land.

Be part of this tale of a surprise partnership amidst the foulest deeds and darkest souls who stalk this peaceful and most beautiful of lands, and you'll never see the Highlands the same way again.

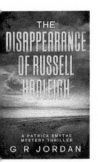

The Disappearance of Russell Hadleigh (Patrick Smythe Book 1)

https://grjordan.com/product/the-disappearance-of-russell-hadleigh

A retired judge fails to meet his golf partner. His wife calls for help while running a fantasy play ring. When Russians start co-opting into a fairly-traded clothing brand, can Paddy untangle the strands before the bodies start littering the golf course?

In his first full novel, Patrick Smythe, the single-armed former policeman, must infiltrate the golfing social scene to discover the fate of his client's husband. Assisted by a young starlet of the greens, Paddy tries to understand just who bears a grudge and who likes to play in the rough, culminating in a high stakes showdown where lives are hanging by the reaction of a moment. If you love pacey action, suspicious motives and devious characters, then Paddy Smythe operates amongst your kind of people.

Love is a matter of taste but money always demands more of its suitor.

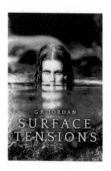

Surface Tensions (Island Adventure Book 1)

https://grjordan.com/product/surface-tensions

Mermaids sighted near a Scottish island. A town exploding in anger and distrust. And Donald's got to get the sexiest fish in town, back in the water

"Surface Tensions" is the first story in a series of Island adventures from the pen of G R Jordan. If you love comic moments, cosy adventures and light fantasy action, then you'll love these tales with a twist. Get the book that amazon readers said, "perfectly captures life in the Scottish Hebrides" and that explores "human nature at its best and worst".

Something's stirring the water!